# YOU ARE WHAT YOU EAT

## DR. SONAL MITTRA

# YOU ARE WHAT YOU EAT

EMBASSY BOOKS
www.embassybooks.in

First Indian Edition 2014
Embassy Books
120 Great Western Building
Maharashtra Chamber of Commerce Lane, Fort
Mumbai - 400 023
India.
www.embassybooks.in

First published 2010
Emerald Publishing, UK

Rajgopal Nidamboor
editor@health-prism.com

ISBN : 978-93-85492-19-8

Cover design: Bookworks Islington, London, UK
Author photograph: Yashwant Rao

# CONTENTS

# Preface

Keshav broke the news to his family members that his company was sending him to India. Everyone was indeed very happy hearing the news especially his Grandmother Sunanda. When Sunanda came to Trinidad from India she was just a 20 years old married to keshav's grandfather who was unemployed. Lot of people from India had migrated to various countries of the world. Sunanda's husband like many others had migrated with his wife to Trinidad. Today after so many years ,on hearing the news of Keshav going to India , Sunanda became nostalgic about her Country and village . The memories of her childhood were still fresh in her mind. While she was unable to accompany Keshav, she asked him to visit Faizpur and meet her relatives for sure.

Keshav stayed with me for a few days and then he wanted to visit his relatives.He wanted me to accompany him  and as I was having holidays I also went along .

Faizpur , a village near Meerut was about half an hour travelling time from there. So the next day having finished the work we reached Faizpur and enquired about his Grandfather and grand uncles. The villagers took us to the village head who happened to be the elder brother of keshav's Grandfather. On seeing his nephew he showered lots of love and affection on him and enquired about the wellbeing of other family members in Trinidad. He told him a lot of interesting stories about his Grandfather and Grandmother which he listened with great interest.

Keshav stayed with his Granduncle. On hearing the news of Keshav's arrival , next day other relatives also came to meet him. He was served curd, lassi ,fruits and parathas for breakfast. Though Keshav was huge and heavy, he was surprised to see that these people had good appetite yet they were slim and trim. Keshav was not used to such kind of breakfast and requested for bread. He told his uncle that since he was overweight he only has a slice of bread and that to without butter, and avoided parathas and the likes. He was surprised to hear what Keshav said. He told him that bread was not good for health and what transpired between them was something like this :-

Keshav - Uncle, abroad everyone has bread ,cheese, jam etc etc for breakfast.

Grand Uncle - That is why most of the people there are obese.

Keshav - why? is it not good to have bread?

G. Uncle - Bread is made out of refined flour which on entering the intestines gets stuck and does not come off easily. Excessive consumption of which leads to constipation.(While he was explaining to Keshav he saw a young girl who was not eating anything and called for her)

Uncle - Suman Beti, what happened why are you not eating your breakfast?

Suman - Uncle, I am suffering from constipation and don't feel like having anything.

Uncle - Take this ripe banana and have lots of water, and you will be alright.

Keshav - Looking astonished, Uncle she will be cured by eating banana?( and he laughs).

Uncle - Yes, bananas have lot of properties. It is very good for the stomach and is good for constipation. (Having said this he takes Keshav to his fields)

After a couple of hours when they returned from the fields they saw cheerful Suman coming towards them.

Uncle - Suman how are you feeling now?

Suman - Uncle , I am relieved and feeling much better now. However, Uncle, Bittoo is down with dysentery and is feeling very weak.

Uncle - Give him a little raw banana.

Keshav - Looking puzzled, Uncle, you asked Suman to eat a banana when she was suffering from constipation and you asked Bitto to have a banana as well while he was suffering from dysentery, how come ?

Uncle - My dear, you did not pay attention, I asked Suman to have a ripe banana whereas I asked Bittoo to be given a raw banana.

Keshav - Are you sure that both will be cured? By eating bananas? No medicines at all?

Uncle - Suman has already been cured, and by tomorrow Bittoo too will be fine. You are here and you see for yourself.

Bittoo - Not convinced , Without medicines ?

Uncle - Son, here the diet is used as a medicine. The lesser we consume the medicines, the better it is for our health and body.

Keshav was still not convinced and more than that was surprised to know all this, and eagerly awaited to meet Suman and Bittoo the next day to know their welfare.

Next day again the Granduncle took Keshav to the

fields. Keshav too started enjoying the fresh air of the village. Keshav once again started the topic of the properties of banana again.

Keshav - Uncle banana is a wonderful fruit, is it true that if we regularly consume bananas we will never have constipation or dysentery?

Uncle - Keshav its not like this, While they were conversing, some one called out , '' its good that I met you here Uncle, infact I was coming to meet you.''

Uncle - What happened, how come you thought of me, I hope all is well?

Person - Last night my wife dropped boiling water on her hand and I applied turmeric paste on the affected part. In fact I wanted to know from you if you would recommend any other herbal medicine for her so that she recovers faster?

Uncle - You did the right thing by applying the turmeric paste, however, let me see the wound

The man took Uncle to his house and called his wife to show her wound. On examining the wound he said that the wound will heal up by two three days.

Person - Uncle how do I prevent the boils from erupting?

Uncle - Apply the paste after every four hours. By evening the pain will subside and there will be no redness around the area as well. Also do give her milk with a pinch of termeric to drink for a few days.

Having advised the man, Uncle along with Keshav moved towards the fields.

Keshav - Uncle, will the burn injury be cured by the application of the turmeric paste ? Out there, we apply medicinal cream as also have medicines along with it.

Uncle - Son we have been using the home remedies for centuries. Once your grandfather had haemorrhoids and your great grandfather fed him with papayas for a few days and cured him. He was about 20 years old then.

Keshav - Uncle, in fact I have also started suffering from haemorrhoids and on my return to Trinidad I will get them operated, even the date of surgery has been fixed with the doctor.

Uncle - Its cure is very simple, and if it is in the initial stages it will take just a week to cure , and if the problem has been there for a while, then it will take a month to cured.

Keshav - Really, what medicine will you prescribe ?

Uncle - I am not going to give you any medicines, just the papaya diet, the same which cured your grandfather.

Keshav - ( Surprised ) Impossible ! (Then laughingly says) Uncle, the cure for heamoroids is only

operation. The doctors there have told me so, then how do I believe in what you say. Agreed for minor ailments such remedies may work, but I have to get operated upon.

Uncle - Son why don't you try the home remedy, you are here for three days. I am not going to give you some herbal or such like medicines, in fact I am going to feed you with papayas and that too in the morning.

Keshav - Uncle, I am not averse to fruits. If that is the cure then why not start right away.

Uncle - Well that's it.

Having returned home, Uncle plucked a papaya from the tree and fed it to Keshav. He told him not to consume bread at all. Three four days, he was given bread made with wheat flour and bran and green vegetables. He felt light. Having papaya in the mornings made motions easy. Keshav realised that even the haemorrhoids have started reducing. He decided to stay put there for another 14 days as he had enough time with him. After 20 days Keshav was surprised to see that he was cured of the haemorrhoids.

Having spent so many days in the village with his Uncle and Keshav I learnt a lot about food and its benefits. I still remember the words of his Uncle who often said "You are what you eat". During one month that we spent with Uncle we learnt a lot about food . Many of our eating habits have also changed . Whatever Uncle propagated/explained and later on whatever I practiced on self anf family and also learnt from friends about diet is compiled in this book.

 # CHAPTER 1
# Importance of food

> 'Your food choices affect not only your health, but the health of your children also, who are likely to follow the same pattern. More than that they affect your genes and thus the gene pool of this Earth.'
>
> **Jonh Robbins**

Bela went to stay with her daughter Ria who is working with a multinational company in Bangalore. Ria is sharing a flat with Munmun. Ria's routine is something like this. She gets up in the morning, has a cup of coffee and goes for a jog. Comes back checks her E-mails over a cup of coffee and some biscuits. It takes an hour or so and she gets ready for the office. Before leaving she eats a toast with black tea and she is done with the breakfast. For lunch she goes to the food court which is right down her office and there she eats whatever is available. Sometimes if she is going for a meeting, she skips that too. By the time she is back home it is 9 o'clock. Her maid who comes when she is away to office makes some dal, vegetables, chappati for her and keeps in a Tiffin. Sometimes she eats this food otherwise she goes out with her friends.

Ria often complained about fatigue, headaches and constipation to her mom Bela. She had also become irritable. After coming back from office she is so tired that she does not want to talk to anybody. She was earning so much but still was not enjoying life. Bela told her that she should eat proper food and the answer she got was,' Mom , I eat my breakfast , have my lunch and eat my dinners. Besides this everyday there is some or the other event where I eat cakes, pastries and samosas. I am not like other girls who skip cakes etc to get slim.'

Bela took her to the doctor. Doctor asked Ria about her food habits and routine, which Ria told. The doctor told Ria that this is exactly what she should not be doing. According to the doctor Ria was consuming refined food ( maida and sugar ) most of the time which was depleting her energy . It was main cause for her fatigue and constipation. Only sometimes she was having ghar ka khana that too at night , which the maid cooked at her own convenient time. It was but natural that Ria would have fatigues, headache and constipation. Doctor told her,' Ria we need energy to work, enjoy, and do many other activities . We need energy during our sleep too because our organs never sleep. Our lungs keep breathing, heart keeps working, stomach keeps digesting while we are at rest or sleep. Food helps in growth. In the process of growing up many cells die or damage and new cells keep building up and taking the place of dead cells. Thus food helps in repairing the tissues. Food builds our immunity. It gives us strength to fight the disease germs by building up our immunity. All bodily functions depend upon food to work well. Food is helpful in regulation of digestion, blood circulation, respiration and excretion etc .Food also gives us joy and elevates our moods. Yes there are certain foods such as chocolates which give pleasure.

Refined food such as maida sticks to the walls of the intestines and blocks the process of eliminations of food. It produces gases which cause headaches.

Doctor changed Ria's rountine completley. She started having proper breakfast, lunch, fruits, and dinner. She was also advised to keep some almonds and walnuts in her bag so that whenever she feels hungry she could have that instead of cakes and samosas. Now Ria is free from constipation and headache.

Aren't we all also careless about our food? Food is the last priority in our list of works.

It is believed that at least 45 chemical components and elements are required by human cell to remain healthy. A complete food is that which has all these nutrients to keep our body healthy. Two of these nutrients are water and oxygen. Remaining 43 are classified into main five groups - carbohydrates, proteins, minerals, fats, vitamins. We get these nutrients from animal food and plant food. Lack of nutrients makes us ill and disease prone. When a particular nutrient has been missing from the meals for a long time, the body gets into deficiency disease. Sometimes due to external factors such as fertilizers, a pesticide, preserving food or chemicals used in food, a particular nutrient goes missing. But we do not have control on it. Lack of that nutrient in our body makes us disease prone. Wrong food habits are also a common factor of illness and we should develop healthy eating habits. A well balanced diet along with healthy food habits keeps one healthy.

## Eat right

Have you ever noticed what all you have on your plate when you have your meals? I am not talking about people in metros only , but also about 75% Indians who are living in cities, towns and villages. For breakfast-seeds in any form ( roti, chapati, porridge, dalia, idli, dosa, paratha, bread, upma), for lunch- roti, dal, rice, vegetables ( mainly seeds) and for dinner again - roti, dal, vegetables, rice ( seeds). Evening and morning tea along with biscuits/ samosa/pakora ( seeds). This is our staple diet. Only carbohydrates and nothing else. This should be staple diet of a labourer or farmer who toils the whole day. Are we really eating healthy? You have to think now!

Our diet should constitute three fistfuls of seeds per day. You may divide it accordingly. We must ( include all seeds one by one in it). Add fruits( all fruits), nuts ( walnuts, almonds, pistachio, peanuts, cashew nuts), sprouts ( anti oxidants), some non vegetarian food( if you are a non vegetarian), milk products( butter milk, cottage cheese , milk etc). Not all in a day but divide it according to your choice.

But eat solid food only twice a day ,either morning and afternoon; or afternoon and evening if you plan to have your dinner by 8 PM.

> *Remember three fistfuls of seeds per day  is the right amount of seeds for us.*

Remember we are not working hard physically that is why we have to cut down on solid food. It makes you lazy, sleepy, lethargic because you are not able to digest it properly. Then you run for tea and coffee to remain active.

> *Each morsel we take in our stomach, works towards our good or bad health.*

Each human being is unique and different and thus has different food requirements. A person who is working in the fields (farmers) requires more nutrition than someone who is on a desk job. A growing child requires all types of food and in substantial quantity, where as a person above forties needs food with less calorific value. As we age the quantity and the types of food varies . For the older lot  fruits, Juices and  less oily and fried stuff is recommended.

We all have different biochemistries and different metabolism, this is all the more a reason we should go for the food which suits us. It will keep us healthy and fit. Our modern lifestyle , development in food industry and copying the west has led us to consume wrong kinds of food. Our diet has also changed drastically. With our lives having got extremely busy we end up grabbing a quick bite in the form of bread and jam in the morning, pizzas , burgers or any other fast food during lunch and oily, fried food , alcohol during very late night dinners. Remember Ria was doing the same thing?  The taste buds of our younger generation make them opt for  beef burger, pork steak, lamb chops and mutton cutlets which is not fresh food but processed food. Noodles, pastas, potato chips, ice creams, chocolate mousse, chilly chicken, mutton roast  isn't all this part of our daily meals?

## Are we really hungry?

Leena is always chewing something or the other throughout the day. You ask her Leena what are you eating? Her answer will be,' nothing yaar, aisi hi, thodi peanuts moonh mein daal li. Or vaise to mein chocolate khati nahi, par subhi ne itne pyar se di mein mana nahi kar saki, Or mein yeh jara taste kar rahi thi.' Leena's weight is 75 KG. she keeps cribbing about her weight and keep saying ,' I hardly eat, par mera to weight hi kum nahi hota.'

Many of us are also doing exactly the same thing. We should listen to our body. We eat anything and at any time of the day. We eat because we are getting bored or somebody had given you a box of chocolates on Deewali , or yesterdays cake is lying in the fridge. And many times cause it is lunch time according to the wall clock, it is 1:30 or 2:00 PM. sometimes we may not be hungry, but still we eat because we like that particular food and have appetite for it. Chaat , Samosa, chocolate, cakes, binging at anything, all this is satisfying our appetite and not our hunger. Psychologically we feel hungry and are tempted to eat to fulfil our desires. And sometimes we may be eating right foods, but eating at wrong time of the day All this results in deterioration of our health because our body has to work more throughout the day to digest whatever we eat. Eating throughout the day is an unhealthy practice . Only hunger fills our stomach.

*Ideal times are : breakfast between 7 to 9 AM, lunch between 12 to 2 PM, a light snack only if you feel hungry at 4 PM and dinner between 6:30 9:30 (2 hours before you sleep).*

*Next time you put anything into your mouth, think twice - 'Are you really hungry?'*

Food should be not only for our body, but it should tickle our mind and soul also. It should nourish us completely. It should keep us healthy.

## Food- body, mind and soul

"To receive the most subtle particles in the food, you must be fully conscious, wide awake, and full of love.

If the entire system is ready to receive food in that perfect way, then the food is moved to pour out its hidden riches when food opens itself, it gives you all that it has in the way of pure, divine energies."

**O. M. Aivanbov**

Amita was waiting for Pavan who promised her that he would come home early as it was Amita's birthday. But when he was about to leave his office some very important client arrived . Pavan's boss told him to stay back as they were having an urgent meeting. Pavan had to arrange lot many things and he called up Amita ,to say that he would be late. Amita took pains to cook delicious meal. When he arrived home it was past midnight and Amita was fuming. They had a hot argument. Amita started raking up the past for the umpteenth time . This infuriated Pavan for this issue had been discussed innumerable times. He tried to pacify her but to no avail. Feeling helpless Pavan poured a drink for himself and seeing this she left everything on the table and went to sleep. Finally what was the result Pavan turned towards alcohol and Amita remained hungry. Both had bad mood for next one week.

In order to lead a happy life we must forget the past and enjoy the present to make the future bright.  On ground it does not happen, we don't do it. We have seen in Amita's case. We need to have a balanced approach on a particular aspect. We should be concious of what we do because we have to reap what we sow. Our karma comes back to us. Too much of krodh, ahamkar , kaam , lobh should be shunned. Metabolic changes in the human body are a continuous process. The human body undergoes transformation every seven years. Our habits thus can change accordingly and we must try to develop good habits.

To lead a happy life there should be balance between body , mind and soul. A healthy body , sound mind can only fulfil this purpose. Healthy body has a positive influence on our mind which further leaves a positive influence on soul. Same way a sound mind will lead us to have healthy food. If there is no harmony in our body, mind and soul, come what may, we will not feel good about ourselves rather will feel low. Our conscious mind is the one which sends signals to different parts of the body. So we should be aware about the health of our mind.

> *The human body undergoes transformation every seven years.*

For our body to function well we should treat it well with balanced diet, sleep and exercise. Here we will talk about diet. Each body is different and thus has different requirements. But still there are a few rules to follow. We should avoid foods and liquids with toxins. As it is these days foods are full of artificial chemicals, pesticides and other kind of adulteration. It can alter our metabolism and dramatically disrupt the body's finely balanced neurotransmitters and hormones leading to altered moods, depression. In the long run, if not treated, can lead to many serious physical problems. To much hatred, anger are results of wrong kind of food which is tamasik.

Our supermarkets are loaded with foods which are adulterated with preservatives, stabilizers, antioxidants, flour treatment agents, thickeners, raising agents, modified starches, emulsifiers, flavour enhancers, artificial sweeteners, acidity regulators, artificial colourings, hydrolyzed proteins etc. Every additive is not bad, some such as calcium ascorbate which is vitamin C, is not bad. But we should avoid others. Some of them like colas etc can give you diseases like depression, panic attacks, heart problems, hair fall and neurological problems.

Thus you see the effect of food on your body and mind both. If body is not healthy, surely your mind is also depressed. Deterioration of body leads to emotional problems. Your emotions are a product of your health. Thus we see that diet has powerful impact on mind through body. There is definitely strong connection between food and mood. Let me explain it. Carbohydrates raise our blood sugar levels soon after we consume it, but it happens for some time and shortly the sugar level drops. That means we gain energy only for a short time. Orexin, a chemical found in our brain becomes inhibited when the blood sugar levels are high and leaves us lethargic, irritable and tired. Emotionally also we feel week. We crave for food again, we indulge in eating sugar based products and the cycle goes on. To get rid of all this we should have a balanced diet i.e complex carbohydrates, proteins and other kinds of food. Bad and irritable mood makes the mind dull and our thinking power is also affected. If body is sick and mind is dull , the souls cannot be happy and blissful. Our body is a vehicle and mind is steering for the soul to achieve enlightenment in this world. If our body functions properly then only the harmony between body, mind and soul can be created. To keep this balance we should not disturb the natural rhythms of our body.

Our diet plays an important role in how we feel. There are foods that can boost our spirit and mind and are good for our body at the same time. People who are spiritually inclined eat certain kinds of foods. They get aversion to certain kinds of foods such as tea, coffee and too much of sugar.

Food is that dynamic force which interacts with human beings on three levels, on physical -body level, the mind-emotional level and energetic-spiritual level.

> 'Health is a state of complete harmony of the body,mind and spirit. When one is free from physical disabilities and mental distractions, the gates of soul open'
>
> **- B.K.S.Iyenger**

Food has effect on our mood, emotions and feelings.

Our health also depends on how we eat, what we eat, how much we eat and when we eat. We should have a balanced diet. All food philosophies agree with this view.

To be in balanced state of mind we have to be at peace with ourselves. Do all your duties well. Spend quality time with your family, mingle with people, do good deeds. Create happiness around yourself. There is definite connection between food and soul, so when you eat be calm, appreciate food and when you sit down to eat, do this with love in your heart. All these things influence our thoughts and mind. Eat Satvik food which keep us calm and cool. This is called holistic eating and total nutrition. This kind of nutrition heals our body, mind and soul.

Someone has rightly said,' we become what we eat! '

Mastication of the food is very necessary. 'Eat slow and chew well' is the mantra of healthy eating. This helps in digestion process.

The size of your stomach depends upon you. If you eat more, your stomach size also increases.( you can develop this thought)

# The Power of Food

> 'All diseases are caused by chemicals and all diseases can be cured by chemicals. All the chemicals used by the body are taken through food. If only we knew about them , all diseases could be prevented and could be cured through their proper use.'
>
> **Dr. Tom Douglas**

Have you ever thought what food can do for you? What are the powers of food we eat?

We talked about relationship between food and body, mind, soul. Food gives us pleasure, peace and elevates our moods. Happiness, prosperity, money and other things we can enjoy only if our health is good and this depends a lot on the food we eat.

My grandmother was very particular that we ate all kinds of foods. My brother did not like papaya but she always insisted that he has papaya early morning. But as soon as she was out of sight, he used to pass it on to us. He was very fond of non-vegetarian food , colas and pizzas. Once he was suffering from constipation and was not eating well at all. My grandmother was not ready to believe it. She said that he has been eating papaya daily that is why there is no reason that he should be constipated. At this time my brother replied,' sorry Da'ma, I never used to have papaya, but pass it on to my sister. 'My grandma started feeding him with papaya every morning with her own hands and within a short time he was relieved of constipation. He also learnt the usefulness of fruits and vegetables. Now he makes it a point that his children have all types of fruit and vegetables.

Even healthy food if consumed in excess and at a wrong time can lead to many lifestyle diseases. If we indulge in wrong kind of food and develop wrong food habits we will certainly get into health problems. Right food can keep us active throughout the day, feeling hungry, thirsty, being tension free and above all having a glowing skin even if the complexion is dark or fair. In addition to the food, a good sleep at the end of the day is a must. Today if you look around, you will hardly see people with these traits. Rather you will find obese, dull and short statured persons around us. Puberty at eight/ten, early menopause, sleep disorders ,vitamin deficiencies, heart attack at twenty, obesity, diabetes, heart attack  cancer at an early age, tension and headache are common things these days. That is what wrong food can do.

> "Let food be thy medicine and medicine be thy food"
> *- Hippocrates*

Lifestyle diseases can be prevented and controlled with a regulated diet. If from childhood, eating healthy should be made part of life, then many diseases can be kept at bay. Nature has given us many such foods that are very effective to keep us rejuvenated and naturally healthy. There are foods which de -stress us , garlic is good for a healthy heart, pea is high in contraceptives, soya is good in reducing triglycerides and cancer risk, carrots are high in carotene, papaya and banana help in regulating bowl movement , turmeric is antiseptic . There are foods which make us more intelligent, improve our immunity and elevate our moods. We should make use of the full power of food. We all know that citrus fruits are used in the cure of scurvy and cod liver oil is used in the cure of rickets.

Food is treated as an important healing force in ayurvedic, Chinese and other philosophies of the world.

# CHAPTER 2
# Food philosophies

> 'He can alone remain healthy, who regulates his diet, exercise and recreation, controls his sensual pleasures, who is generous, just , truthful and forgiving, and who gets along well with his relatives.'
>
> ***( Ayurveda)***

The other day one of my friends rang up to find out what is liquorice and ginseng. Her son who is studying in an international school came home and asked her about ginseng and liquorice. When she asked him why he wants to know. His answer was that his friend Cheng , who is also studying in the same class eats lot of liquorice that is why his voice is so good . And he sings very well. He is powerful because his mother gives him ginseng( All this Cheng told him). I explained to her that liquorice is something like Indian mulethi and ginseng is a very potent Chinese herb.

Another friend of mine prepared Mediterranean food when she called me for dinner. She had cooked ( read deep fried) Salmon in olive oil. I had a heart to tell her that olive oil is not meant for deep frying. These days world has really shrunk and become just like one small village. Lot of knowledge is freely available on internet , out of which some is researched and some without researched. We do not know what is correct and what is not. Chinese food, Tibetan, Thai, Mexican, Italian, Japanese, Mediterranean food is available everywhere. Each type of food has something good for the health and at the same time because of modern life style many things are added in it later on to make it more tasty which may be making it harmful.

There are many kinds of food philosophies prevailing from time immemorial to this day. Ayurvedic philosophy, Chinese philosophy, Greek philosophy, Tibetan philosophy etc. Let's know about different food philosophies first.

## Ayurvedic Philosophy

Ayurveda the Oldest philosophy of healing originated from Atharvaveda , which is as old as 100 B.C. Ayurveda does not deal with medicines only , it deals with everything related to life. Ayurveda means knowledge of life. Life is a combination of body, mind and soul.

Ayurveda means science of life. The philosophy of ayurvedic food is based upon the priciple that there should be unity among everything which exists in this universe. The whole universe is made up of five elements: ether, air, fire, water and earth. These five elements are dependent on each other. Ether, the first element is space and everything exists in space. Nothing exists without space. The second element in order is air which exists in space. Third element fire exists because of ether and air. Existence of the fourth element water depends upon all first three. The fifth element earth contains all other four elements and is the heaviest among all.

All these five elements are also present in our body. Our body is made of these five elements that is why it is called Panch bhuta shareer. They are in the form of three humours ( tridosha) which are vata, pitta and kapha. When any of the doshas accumulate more than the desired limit, body loses its balance. In a healthy person all three doshas( humour) are in a balanced state. A healthy person feels hungry, cheerful and good spirited. Place (desh), time (kaal), climate, food, age, mental stage all affects the balance in these three doshas. Here we will strict ourselves to food only.

## Theory of tridosha or bio-energies:-

Vata- formed with ether and air.

Pitta- formed with fire

Kaphs- formed with water and earth.

**Vata:-** Vata consists of ether and air. This energy is seen as force which is responsible for all body movements, nerve impulses, blood circulation, respiration, excretion, sensation, hearing ,speech ,sexual act and natural urges.

**Pitta:-** This energy pertains to fire and water. It governs our metabolism. It transforms food into energy. It is responsible for hunger, thirst, vision, heat, intellect, softness, luster and cheerfulness.

**Kapha:-** Consists of water and earth. It governs the solid structure of the body, its growth and protection. It is responsible for firmness, heaviness, sexual potency, and strength and binding. The cerebral-spinal fluid that protects the brain and spine are all governed by kapha.

You must have noticed that some of your friends are healthy and some are slim, weak and fall sick easily. This is because Every human being is different from the other because of his fundamental constitution. In some of them one energy will be predominant while the others may have different energy predominant. And it may be in a different percentage. Raw tomato may be good for you and may not be good for your sister.

As discussed earlier place (desh), time (kaal), climate, food, age and mental stage etc all affect the balance in these three doshas. **(Butter milk may not suit a person staying on hill stations, whereas it will be beneficial for a person residing in hot place such as Jaipur or down south in Chennai.)** We also have three qualities of mind which are present in our food. They are rajas, tamas and sattva or we can say rajasik, tamasik and sattavik. The rajasik mind thinks , planes and takes decisions. Tamasik mind hinders growth and motion of mind. It is greedy, jealous and lethargic. Sattavik mind is truthful, compassionate and peaceful. There should be balance among these three also. There balance influences balance of the three humours (doshas) and can cause mental problems if it is imbalance.

Thus to maintain a healthy and long life there should be six dimensional equilibrium, i.e. three humours and three gunas (qualities of mind). These three humours (doshas)of the body and the three qualities of the mind keep changing constantly subjected to our way of life. If any kind of imbalance occurs we can set it right through food. All the five elements found in nature and our body are also found in food. They are traced through six rasas or tastes in our food. Each rasa is derived from two elements. These six rasas are sweet, sour, salty, pungent, bitter and astringent. Our body can detect sweet rasa quickly.

Sweet – water and earth. It reduces vata and pitta and promotes kapha.

Sour- Fire and water. It pacifies vata and promotes pitta and kapha.

Salt- Fire and earth. It reduces vata and promotes pitta and kapha.

Pungent- Air and fire. It reduces kapha and promotes vata and pitta.

Bitter- Ether and air. It promotes vata and reduces kapha and pitta.

Astringent-Air and earth. It enhances vata and reduces pitta and kapha.

These are general guidelines.

Radish (mooli) when in tender stage controls all three rasas but when it is fully ripe it aggravates all three rasas and hence it is not good to eat a fully ripe mooli.

Each rasa has specific therapeutic values. These rasas help in digestion and affect its metabolism. Minor disorders caused by the imbalance of these doshas can be cured by diet. We must incorporate all six tastes in our food so that we can have healthy and tasty food with all five five elements in it. Sometimes because of travelling or change of place any one humour becomes imbalanced, in that case by changing our diet we can bring back the balance. Hence diet should be changed according to place, climate, time and situation.

## Three states ( qualities, gunas) of Food-

As we have three states of mind, which is called trigunas, we also have three states of food, sattavic, rajasik and tamasic.

After food is digested a substance called 'Ojas' is extracted from food. Ojas is responsible for proper functioning of mind and spiritual development of a person. According to ayurveda, before consuming food we should give proper attention to the state of food and effect of food on our body. The most important thing is that food energy should flow through the seven tissue layers of our body.

**Sattavic Food:-** Pure vegetarian food, which is freshly cooked is called Satvik food. It includes fruits, vegetables, grains, milk, ghee and pulses. This kind of food is easily digested and brings balance to our mind. It builds immunity and has healing properties. Sattavik food keeps us healthy. It is devoid of preservatives and additives. It raises our consciousness, inspires us to do good, think positive and be spiritual. It brings out our hidden potentials and makes us creative. It is devoid of chillies and black pepper, though one can use green chillies. Common spices such as cinnamon, coriander, aniseed, cardamom salt and turmeric are used in it. Not all raw food is sattvik. Tomato, carrots and salads are sattvik food.

This kind of food is freshly cooked and eaten when it is still fresh and warm. It is cooked with love and care. Whatever is cooked yesterday should not be consumed today. It will not remain sattvik. Sattvik food makes a person calm and poised. It builds immunity and keeps a person healthy. He who eats sattvik food is balanced in his thinking, habits and approach towards life.

> *Freshly cooked food gives us more energy and nutrients than stale food. Any cooked food after 8 hours becomes stale.*

**Rajasik Food: -** Rajasik food may be cooked freshly but it does not get digested easily. This kind of food is hot, spicy, pungent, oily, fried and over sweet. Garlic and many other plant roots also fall in this category. People who require lot of energy and do physical hard work should eat this kind of food because they are able to digest it. It may give us energy for that moment but eventually it will give us stress. This kind of food gives aggression and sensual stimulation. It destroys the body and mind balance.

Though it is high in quality but deficient in nutrients. All sweets (mithai), ice cream, cakes ,pastries are rajasik food.

Have you seen any person around you who is very active, does all his jobs in a hurry, rushes through food ? loves power and wants to enjoy life? Though he has full control over his life but his own health is out of his hands? He will always feel bloated and heavy? Your answer will be in affirmative. There are thousands around us who fall in this category. they all are Rajasik. They have poor digestion and health because of this.

**Tamasic Food:-** Tamas means darkness .Tamasik food is dead food such as meat, chicken, fish, eggs etc. All stale food which has been cooked more than 8 hours before falls under tamasik food. All kinds of liquor, wine, refined flour, refined sugar, caffeine, pickles etc come under this kind of food. Modern junk foods, pizzas, colas which make us fatty are part of tamasic food. If sattvik food is processed, it will become tamasik food. It affects our nervous system and heart. It requires lot of energy to digest sattvik food. Many life style diseases generates because of tamasic food. It does not give us energy rather it makes us lethargic and lazy. Tamasik food leads us to many health problems such as obesity, heart problems, diabetes and cancer etc. it makes a person dull. Tamasik people are self-centered and not bothered about others. They have no regard for anybody else. They suffer from imbalance in life and age very fast. This kind of food makes you loose control on your appetite and you tend to eat each and everything.

Do not go by the name only. We require all three types of food to be in balance state. If there was no tamas guna, we would not be able to sleep. Lack of tamasik food produces sleep disorders and insomnia. Making onions part of your diet is recommended for such disorders. Without sattva guna there would not be inspiration and spiritualism for us. And without rajas guna we would not be working actively. Hence three qualities ( gunas) of food have influence on our physical, mental, emotional and spiritual health.

**Age factor:-** During childhood (upto 16 years) kapha energy is more predominant in the body. Kapha element forms the body's solid structure. It is period of growth for a child. Because kapha element suppresses pitta element, babies require pitta elements also. For this we should give food which has fire element in it.

Childhood is followed by youth (16 to 40 years), when pitta energy prevails in the body. Fire element in the body becomes predominant. So food rich in fire element should be consumed in less quantity. It will aggrevate pimples and other age related problems. Bitter rasa dominant foods should be consumed at regularly to prevent problems of pitta elements.

In the old age, above 40 years, vata element is more dominant in the body. People do not change their food habits. We all have seen that people in old age start having vata related problems such as joint pains, insomnia and wind related problems etc. That is why it is very important to eat according to one's age.

> *Must sit in vjra -asana for 5-10 minutes, after having your meals. The food gets digested easily. The gas formation in the stomach also becomes slow. This is the only asana which can be done immediately after the meals. To see the result start from today only.*

**Time of the day:-** Kapha prevails in the morning and evening from 6 A.M. to 10 A.M. and 6 P.M. to 10 P.M.

10 A.M. to 2 P.M. and 10 P.M. to 2 A.M is pitta predominant time. Rest of the time vata remains dominant.

Food which is predominantly cold should not be consumed at night during winters. Same way food with more of pitta elements should not be consumed on a hot summer day.

**Time of the year:-** It is important to keep in mind the seasons of the year. During summers human body is different from what it is in winters. Summers are pitta dominant time. So pitta dominant foods should be avoided during summers. During summers curd, rice, lentils, green vegetables should be consumed. Lot of liquids and salads should be part of our meal. Light and easily digestible foods such as bottle guard should be consumed.

Dry, cold winters are vata dominant time. So vata and kapha dominant foods should not be consumed during winters. Winter foods are sweet, acidic and salty. During winters our digestion power is at its maximum so easy-to-digest foods should be avoided during winter.

Kaphas dominates during hot and humid weather and hence kapha dominant foods should be avoided during this weather. During rainy season bitter guard should be eaten as it purifies the blood. Foods which are pungent, bitter and astringent should not be consumed.

Still if one wants to consume some particular kind of food, then lot of condiments and other accompaniments should be added. For example kidney beans and mustard leaves cause all three doshas, yet they are largely consumed in Punjab with lot of onion, garlic, ginger, ghee and other condiments in it so that the doshas get neutralized.

## Ayurvedic norms:-

Some foods are hot and some cold according to ayurveda. Hot foods promote pitta element in the body and cold foods create vata or kapha. There are a few foods which have balanced equilibrium. These foods should be consumed often. Foods which are not balanced should be made balanced by adding some herbs and spices of the opposite element. People with pitta constitution have more heat in their body. They should use, coriander, aniseed, curd, in their diet. Lactating mothers should add dried ginger, cumin seeds, cottage cheese, moong dhuli dal in their diet as it increases the flow of milk. A person with cold constitution or kapha dominance should avoid curd at night. A person with hot constitution should not have potatoes. If it is necessary then add coriander, saunf and a little curd in it.

This way one should keep the balance by adding food from all energies. That is why in India so many herbs and spices are added while cooking food.

> If you have consumed unbalanced food unknowingly in a party, you should take ajwain, rock salt and lime with warm water. You will feel ok.

## Remember everything which is in balance is good for you.

## Rules:-

Don't we get fed up by eating one kind of food daily? Yes , we do. That is why nature has produced a large variety of food for us which is different in taste, shape, and sizes. There are six rasa in natural food and all six rasa should be included to the diet. Only any one rasa should not be dominant in our food. If all rasa are included in food, it creates ojas . Ojas gives us energy and vitality. Generally bitter rasa has been seen missing from many menus. Make sure to include it at least once a day. Include a variety of vegetables in your food. Try to have seasonal fruits and vegetables. They are more nutritious and less costly during their particular season. Food eaten while you are standing, walking or in a state of anger can give you health related problems. So do not eat when you are under stress. Before starting your meal your entire mind should be thinking about your meal. Do not drink water during eating. Have water half an hour after eating your food. If it is very necessary to have water during meals have it in sips only. Juices should not be taken along with the meal. Take juice half an hour before the meal. Same way curd should be eaten first thing while eating. Let the previous food digest before you plan to have next meal. Nothing should be taken between the meals. Body has to digest everything taken in. Do not take bath after eating. Do this before eating. Otherwise it will cool down digestive juices and our system has to work more. If you remember and follow these rules your health can never trouble you.

## Chinese Philosophy

Traditional Chinese Food Philosophies are derived and guided by traditional Chinese Medicine theories. For them **Food Is Medicine**. They believe that food, seasons, weather and nature all affect human beings. Their dietary guidelines are followed from nature. If we eat food which is seasonal and in harmony with our environment then we can adapt better to the changes in season and remain in harmony with nature and thus remain healthy. This statement is based on 'yin, yang and qi' principle. Emperor Shen Nong (3000 BC) developed the theory of Yin, Yang and qi. According to this theory everything in this universe is either Yin –cold, dark and introverted or Yang- hot, bright and extroverted or qi which is energy. Yin and yang represent opposites but dependent forces. Food is also classified into Yin and Yang depending on whether hot or cold. Even our body parts too are divided same way. Yin foods being cold have chilling effect and Yang foods have warming effect on our bodies or on qi (energy). During summer and spring we should nourish yang and during autumn and winter we should nourish yin. We require having both types of foods to keep balance in our body. If we consume too much of one kind of food, then imbalance is created in the body and we fall sick. Sometimes a particular organ suffers with deficiency of Yin or Yang which can be corrected with appropriate foods.

> *In 3000 B.C. Chinese Emperor used to honour first soybean sowing. Ginseng used to be weighed even in gold sometimes. That says how good Ginseng is.*

They also believed that there are 5 elements in the universe-earth, fire, water, metal and wood and all living beings fall under one category. According to them food is also categorized under these elements and so are our body parts. We should not consume too much or too little food from one category. Because deficiency of certain foods may create imbalance and make the corresponding organ weak.

For them food should be consumed to keep us healthy and cheerful. It should give us energy. It should increase our qi( life -force). To maintain balance, health and energy level we should have fresh and seasonal food.

Yin organs store body materials such as blood, fluid and qi( energy) and Yang controls functions. Any organ which suffers from some problem can be cured by related yin or yang food type.

| Yin | Yang |
| --- | --- |
| Heart | Gall bladder |
| Spleen | Small intestine |
| Lungs | Large intestines |
| Kidney | Bladder |
| liver | Stomach. |

The Yin and Yang food is given below. Very general breakdown of Yin, Yang and neutral food is given here.

| Yin Foods:- | Yang Foods:- | Neutral Foods:- |
|---|---|---|
| vegetables, fruits, sea food | beef, lamb, eggs, duck | rice, noodles, whole grains, kidney beans. |

Chinese food also has concept of flavours which are of five types- sweet, sour, salty, bitter and pungent. All food is divided among these flavours.

1. **Sweet flavours:-** potato, wheat, licorice, pea, honey, sweet potato , banana etc

2. **Sour flavours:-** lemon, tomato, grapes, apple, pomegranate, tamarind etc.

3. **Salty flavours:-** salt, barley, millet, kelp etc.

4. **Bitter flavours:-** orange peel, coffee, bittergaurd, karaunda etc

5. **Pungent flavours:-** ginger, garlic, pepper, onion, leeks etc.

Chinese food because of its different flavours has specific type of effect on human beings. Pungent flavours open the pores of our skin and causes perspiration. For example-ginger and garlic which is used for cough and cold. Sour flavoured foods such as lemon are used to help in loose motions. For curing weakness instantly we use sweet flavours.

Hence we see that in Chinese food philosophy also food plays a great role in curing a person. More emphasis is on natural fresh food with its natural flavours.

**By the way, Chinese food which we eat in India is poor version of Chinese food. Rather I will say that it is not even**

Indochinese food. It is neither Indian nor Chinese, God only knows what it is.

## Greek Philosophy

Let thy food be thy medicine and thy medicine be thy food.'

**Hippocrates**

That means food and medicine are not two different things, they are one and the same. Then where is the difference? Food and medicines both are made from herbs and plant extracts. Food also has therapeutic properties but milder than medicines. It has more of nutrition. Same way medicine has less nutrition and more therapeutic properties. Food philosophy in ancient Greek had two basic ideas. Food should be consumed to maintain overall health. Have fresh food, on regular intervals and do not overeat. The other is food should manage any sickness or disease. This is consumed for limited time period, which is meant for therapeutic objectives. Managing patient's diet is an essential part of the treatment of the patient.

Greek, Chinese and Ayurvedic diet therapies have many things in common. They believe in harmonizing the health of individuals with nature. Fresh food is the bases of their diet. Food is consumed to keep humours in balance. If there is excess of cold in the body, then ginger, garlic or honey is given to the suffering person to nullify cold with heat in body. To keep the body humours in balance, Greek physicians use food along with herbs. food has its own temperament like hot, cold food etc. All the food is divided in four humours and it influences

41

functions of our body.

> *Bible has a mention of barley, honey, curd, cheese, grapes at many places. Olives are considered as staple food in Greece. olives are good in any form.*

Right food item should be selected to cure particular ailment. For example, pears and horseradish both are used in chronic lung and respiratory problems. Horseradish is hot and spicy in temperament and used for clearing phlegm and congestion from lungs. Whereas pears are cooling and moistening in temperament and are used in condition of lung heat and dryness.

Alfalfa and comfrey is good for bones and joints, watermelon, blackberry, currants, fenugreek, cucumber all are good for kidney and urinary problems. The list is unending and will be discussed later in this book.

In traditional cooking they believe in flavours and using fresh ingredients. Lot of olive oil is used. Lot of greens such as oregano, mint, dill, bay, thyme, basil, fennel, onion, garlic and ginger is used. Greek salads are world famous. All these herbs are very much used in Indian cooking also. They consume lot of fresh vegetables, fruits, curds, honey, fish and tomatoes. Their basic grain is wheat and also barley. Greek honey is extracted from fruit trees and citrus trees.

Greeks believe in eating together and sharing food, they have named it' Paraia'. The tall white hats which the chef's wear have originated in Greece. In middle ages, monks who used to prepare food in Greek monasteries used to wear tall white hats so that that they could be distinguished from the other monks.

Note:-

1. Olive oil is monounsaturated fat which is called a healthy fat. It can lower the LDL( bad) cholesterol , FDA also recognized that olive oil can help reduce heart disease risk, we can use it in place of other fats.

2. Greek philosopher Aristotle used to cook lentils with saffron. Lentils are considered to have aphrodisiacal properties.

3. Hippocrates, Greek physician believed that consuming mint makes a person feels tired and lethargic.

4. Alexander had given instructions to his men not to have mint tea while going to a war, as it induced sexual desires.

> There is an Island in Greece named Island of Ikaria in Aegean Sea, where people have the longest life spans in the world. They consume plant based diet, olive oil, whole wheat, fish, goat milk .

## Tibetan philosophy

Tibetan philosophy of food is based on natural and holistic way which deals with human need to be connected to body, mind and soul. It is deeply rooted in culture and spirit of Tibetans. Different types of food have different effects on human body, mind and soul. They believe that food is to keep us healthy. For this they give lot of emphasis on correct diet and lifestyle, which is fundamental to Traditional Tibetan Medicine also.

If one falls sick, the prominent treatment should be to change the diet of the patient. Rest of the treatments should supplement diet changes. If diet change does not work then only some other treatment should be followed. To be healthy an emphasis should be on balancing the stomach. They believed in light eating and not filling the stomach to full. One should fill the stomach with 50% solid, 25% fluids and 25% space, so that whatever is eaten can be mixed easily in the stomach. They believe in having warm water and cold water. Food should be digested properly. The stagnant food in our stomach is the root cause of all problems related to health. For this, we should leave ¼ of our stomach empty while eating. (similar to Indian and Chinese philosophy.)

> *Raw vegetables and raw fruits should not be eaten at the same time as both require different types of enzymes for their digestion.*

They believed in three humors i.e wind, bile and phlegm and five elements i.e space, air, fire, earth and water. Once any imbalance arises between them, we fall sick and it becomes necessary to cure the balance first. Balance means harmony between body, mind and soul. Energy is a vital link between body, mind and soul. Energy is that dynamic power which is the source of our and all living beings' existence. It arises from five elements mentioned above. All these have their individual qualities which are shown below in the box. Any imbalance between them result in sickness and is cured by curing this imbalance through diet gives us energy again and we feel healthy.

| Tibetan | Humour | Element | Quality | Functions |
|---------|--------|---------|---------|-----------|
| Tripa | Bile | Fire | Heat | Digestive system, catabolic functions, feeling of hunger, thirst, courage, motivation, heat in body, vision |
| Lung | Wind | Air and Space | Movement | Thought process, mind, nervous system, respiration, excretion |
| Badkan | Phlegm | Earth and water | Solidity, fluidity | Body fluids, body structure, anabolic functions and sleep patterns. |

Now for treating any imbalance or treating the patient, first of all his diet has to be changed which helps in maintaining balance. According to these three humors patient has to adjust his diet. Guidelines are, nutritional diet, natural diet which is low in salt and sugar, fats and meat in moderation , no pickles, preserved foods and drinks , lot of fresh vegetables, lot of liquids , milk, water, rice, all kinds of beans and lot of herbs as drinks etc.

A perusal of all philosophies as highlighted above would reveal that all of them advocate use of fresh food and in moderation for a healthy life. Majority of the ailments are on account of inappropriate eating habits, as also the right food consumed in right measure acts as a healing agent.

**Macrobiotics Diet philosophy :-** Macrobiotics is a Greek word which consists of two words Macro-large and bio-life , so it means large life. Macrobiotics Diet philosophy was developed by George Oshawa a Japanese.

It is a low fat, high fiber vegetarian diet based on consumption of all kinds of whole grains. It is low in meat, meat products, milk, milk products and sugars.

Rules about food:-

1. Rules are based on climate of a place, season of the year, age of the person, gender, type of work he does, his health requirements.

2. Macrobiotic diet consists of whole grains such as wheat, corn, brown rice, barley, millet, rye, buckwheat etc.

3. According to this diet vegetables should be consumed in their raw form.

4. Fermented, boiled, steamed, sautéed, baked foods and soups are recommended in this diet.

5. Soya products must be consumed at least once a day. They may be beans, tofu, soya granules, soya flour, soya chunks, in boiled or cooked form.

6. Seasonal fruits should be consumed everyday. Mango, papaya and pineapple should be avoided.

7. All types of seeds, nuts and dry fruits in their roasted form should be consumed.

8. No animal products except fish. This may be on alternate day of the week

9. Sugars , honey, molasses should be avoided.

10. Sesame oil is very popular in macrobiotic diet. Mustard oil and corn oil can also be used. Oil should be unrefined form.

11. Condiments should be sea salt, rock salt, brown rice vinegar, ginger root.

12. Pickles should be in their fermented form.

Macrobiotic diet has been recommended for cancer and many other chronic diseases. This low fat diet contains phytoestrogen which reduces the risk of cancer. Further researches are going on in this area.

This kind of diet cleans our system by clearing toxins from our nadis( meridians) and keeps us free from sluggishness.

**Caution:- macrobiotic diet according to some people lacks in certain vitamins and nutrients such as Vitamin B 12, calcium and magnesium.**

 # CHAPTER 3
# Composition of Food

> 'When I am eating I am deaf and dumb'.
>
> *- Russia*

Mitali is a young girl of 22 years. Her mother Madhur is a good friend of mine. The other day when we were sitting and chatting at her place, she got a phone call from Mitali's friend that Mitali had become unconscious and is admitted in the hospital. Both of us panicked and reached the hospital. There the doctor asked Madhur about Mitali's food habits and told that Mitali had become highly anemic. She was also developing kidney problems. Mitali suffered from fatigue, headaches and palpitation. She was eating very less, only soups and salads. These days everyone wants to become like famous actor Kareena Kapoor, with size zero and hence stops eating or starts eating very less. They do not realise that by eating soups and salads only they are missing out on other essential nutrients. All these famous actors including Kareena are under the supervision of super specialists for 24 hours. But young girls just see the broad picture and get carried away. The truth is we need these nutrients to give us energy, so that our body functions can be carried out smoothly.

It is believed that at least 45 chemical components and elements are required by human cell to remain healthy. Can we miss out on even one of these nutrients? No, not at all.

Is it possible to omit carbs from our food, or proteins or fats ? no, we have already seen the results. Mitali was doing exactly the same thing.

These nutrients are divided into 5 main categories such as proteins, carbohydrates, fats, vitamins, minerals, enzymes. Some foods have one kind of nutrients and others may have many kinds but may lack in any one. To lead a healthy life we need all the nutrients in our food. We need proteins, carbohydrates, fats in large amounts as they give energy to us . Vitamins and minerals are needed for our body to function well and efficiently for many other functions. Our body is roughly 22% protein, 13% fat, 2% minerals and vitamins and rest 63% water.

**Carbohydrates:-** Their main function is to provide fuel and energy to body. All types of cereals like wheat, corn, jowar, bajra, ragi, rice are carbohydrates. They are called digestible starches. They also provide us bulk which is very essential for our body. Vegetables also contain starch which is called fibre and is indigestible starch. All fibres provide us roughage which helps in eliminating waste from body. Carbohydrates spare the protein to perform other functions. They come in two forms, fast releasing such as sugar, honey, jaggery and refined food and slow releasing or complex carbohydrates like whole grains, vegetables and fruits. Fast releasing carbohydrates slow down our digestion and put unnecessary load on other organs. Complex carbohydrates are good for optimal health than fast releasing.

we should consume carbs in limited amount otherwise they will get stored as fat in our body and we all know how difficult it is to get rid off fat.

**Protein:-** People have very vague ideas about proteins. Many of them think that if they take high protein diet all their health problems will be solved. It is not like that. High protein diet is very essential for growing kids and for those who do strenuous exercises and gimming along with heavy workouts. For rest of us it should be consumed in normal amounts.

Of course they are building blocks of our body and every cell in our body –muscle , bone, blood, brain, skin and hair etc contains protein. All this is very true, but remember, excess of everything is bad.

Proteins are made out of 22 amino acids , only some amino acids are produced in our body and rest we obtain from food .They are divided in two types : indispensible amino acids and dispensable ones. Indispensables are one ones which we should have from diet because our body cannot make them. The other ones are those which our body makes. They are vital for growth and reconstruction of the body cells and tissues. They are also helpful to make hormones, antibodies and enzymes Pluses, lentils, soya, fish meat etc. Non-vegetarian diet consists of all the essential amino acids but all of them are not available in vegetarian food.

The quality of proteins which we eat is very important. It is one of the most important nutrient which is required to break down fat into energy . Animal proteins such as milk, meat, fish, chicken and eggs etc is high quality protein. Eggs protein is the highest in quality, and then comes meat followed by vegetables, cereals and pulses. Sometimes we combine two types of proteins to get maximum results. For example pulses and wheat, rice and pulses. Nuts and dry fruits are also rich source of proteins.

**Note: After water, protein is the substance which is very essential for our body. Its helps in building of body, muscles, tendons, ligaments, nails and hair. It is also helpful to burn off fat in body. Do not consume very high levels of protein as it may deplete calcium from the bones.**

**Fat :-** Nitu is skinny and has good features. But she looks haggard and old with dry and patchy skin. Her dull eyes tell everything about her poor health. She has started feeling pain in her joints. She is very particular about no fat diet , not even a single drop of oil. She takes boiled vegetables, dry chapati ( one which is without ghee), all types of fruit etc. if you tell her about this she has the answer that she takes everything but fat is not required as she will bloat up.

She does not understand that fat is responsible for youthful shining skin and sparkling eyes. When one is under stress ( physical and mental) or is without food for a long period, it is stored fat in the body which helps us survive. Fats are vital for the brain, nervous system and skin. Lack of fats results in dry skin. More fat gives disease like high blood pressure and heart problems.

_Note:- Friends please, switch over to cold pressed oils._

Besides this it also has many other functions in our body. It provides heat and energy to our body. It helps in utilization of many vitamins such as Vitamin A,D,E,K. It protects our vital organs and works as protective sheath.

Most important , it lubricates the joints. There are two types of fat saturated and unsaturated fat. Sources of getting fat are plants and animal food. Vegetable fat is better digested by our body. Animal fats contain saturated fatty acids which become cause of cholesterol and blockage in arteries. There are three types of fatty acid. Saturated fatty acids, Mono unsaturated fatty acids and Poly- unsaturated fatty acids.

1. **Saturated fatty acids ( SFA ):-** The saturated fat is solid at room temperature. We get them from Palm oil, coconut oil, dairy products, meats, cocoa butter etc. you should not take in high amounts and regularly. This kind of fat can be harmful eventually.

2. **Unsaturated fatty acids (UFA):-** At room temperature it remains in liquid form . Coconut oil, olive oil , mustard oil are the example . It is further divided into three groups.

   a) **Mono Unsaturated fatty acids (MUFA):-** We get them from olive oil, mustard oil, rapeseed oil, peanut oil , badam oil and fish oil etc.

   *We should never reheat and reuse cooking oils because it oxidizes Poly- unsaturated fats in it, which damages our blood vessels. This oil is equal to poison.*

   b) **Poly unsaturated fatty acids (PUFA):-** We get this kind of fat from sunflower oil, flax seed oil, walnut oil, soya bean oil, linseed oil and fish etc. etc. Mainly we get them from vegetable oils. It contains essential fatty acids (EFA). Some Fatty acids which are essential for us but our body cannot synthesis them, are supplied through food items to us are called essential fatty acids. They help in avoiding vascular damage to our heart and brain by controlling blood pressure, preventing clotting of blood in arteries. It affects women during menstrual cycles and helps contractions during childbirth. They are known as Omega 3 and Omega 6 fatty acids .

**Omega 3 Fatty Acids:-** It protects against heart diseases, high blood pressure, and certain inflammatory and autoimmune disorders. It is also known for lowering triglycerides. You can find Omega 3 fatty acids in pulses like Rajmah , lobia, urad dal ,flaxseeds, walnuts , leafy green vegetables , wheat , bajra, canola oil , mustard oil etc. Fish and eggs are also rich source of this fatty acid.

**Omega 6 Fatty Acids:-** Eggs, whole wheat, cereals and some vegetable oils are rich source of Omega 6 Fatty Acids.

Our diet must contains both omega 3 and omega 6 in equal amount.

c) **Trans fats:-** These days big companies have started converting unsaturated fats into saturated fats by hydrogenation process. This is cheap in cost and is used widely for commercial purpose. It is very harmful for our health. It raises the level of LDL cholesterol.

### Now you know when you eat food out in the restaurants, what kind of food you eat?

We should consume less of saturated fatty acids (SFA) to keep blood cholesterol level low. Consumption of SFA can lead to many other diseases also. Mono unsaturated fatty acids (MUFA) decrease LDL and increase HDL. Oils containing Poly-unsaturated fats can reduce both LDL and HDL ( Bad as well as good) cholesterol.

In fact we should use blended oil instead of any one type.

*Hydrogenation:- Changing any oil from liquid into a solid spread involves the adding of hydrogen atoms to the fatty acid molecule. This is known as hydrogenation. Vegetable oils are subjected to intense heat and pressure in the presence of hydrogen and nickel to produce hydrogenated oils. This process of hydrogenation results in the formation of Trans fatty acids. Food item with hydrogenated oils should be consumed in minimum quantity as they contain saturated fat.*

Nuts like almond, hazelnuts, macadamia nuts are good in MUFA and nuts like walnuts and peanuts are good in PUFA. All nuts are high in fat, except chestnuts. Our daily consumption of nuts should not be more than 30 gm.

> *Flaxseed oil should not be used for cooking as it is easily perishable.*

**Vitamins: -** There has been lot of talk about Vitamins. Though they are required in very small amount, but at the same time are very essential for our body. Vitamins help in processing proteins, carbohydrates and fats etc. so that these elements could perform their function well. They are needed for the process of metabolism in the body. Body cannot produce vitamins (except Vit K), we must get them from other sources. Vitamins are also required to balance hormones, produce energy, boost the immune system, protect the arteries, and are vital for the brain and nervous system. There are many types of vitamins such as vitamin A,B,C,D,E,K,P, Vitamin B1,B2, B6,B12 , Niacin, folate, Vitamin P. vitamins are classified into two groups fat soluble ( A,D,E and K)and water soluble ( Vitamin B group and C).

**Vitamin A:-** It plays a part in the process of seeing. Eyesight depends upon physical attribute, eye lens, and partly on a chemical process involving vitamin A. Lack of Vitamin A causes problem in seeing. All yellow vegetables, egg yolk, milk, curd are rich source of this vitamin. Pumpkin and carrots are very rich source of Vitamin A.

**Vitamin B:-** Required to maintain healthy skin and hair. Builds metabolism, immunity and healthy nervous system. It keeps us happy. There are many types of vitamin B such as B 1, B2, B3, B5, B6, B7, B8, and B12. They all come under Vitamin B or B comlex.

**Vitamin C:-** Remember when we are down with cold , doctor suggests that we must have vitamin c? All citrus fruits are good source of vit c. very good for skin too. But this vitamin is easily lost during chopping and washing of vegetables. That is why we should not make juice and keep it for long time , rather consume it as soon as possible. It is very powerful anti oxidant and immunity booster.

**Vitamin D:-** Our body makes it with the help of sun light. Without this there is no use of calcium because calcium is better absorbed by our body with the help of vitamin D. Next time make it a point to sit in the morning sun at least for 15 minutes.

**Vitamin E:-** it is easily available in all seeds , nuts and vegetables. But over cooking and processing destroys it. That is why they say whole wheat is better than refined wheat (maida). All green leafy vegetables are rich source of this vitamin.

> *Vitamin E prevents fat turning into toxic in our body. So it should be part of our daily diet. All green leafy vegetables, all nuts and seeds are rich source of this vitamin.*

**Vitamin K:-** Many people do not know much about this vitamin. What happens when we get hurt or when our finger is cut while doing something? Blood starts oozing out. And after sometimes on medication it stops also. Who does it? Our very neglected vitamin K. yes it plays major role in clotting of the blood. Any where excessive bleeding means lack of vitamin K. Even women who have excessive bleeding during menstrual cycle, they lack vitamin K.

We cannot even think of omitting even one vitamin from our food.

> *Do not apply vitamin oils such as vitamin E capsules on your skin as our skin cannot absorb these oils. You have to eat them through food. That is the best way.*

**Minerals:-** Minerals and trace elements are as essential to our health as vitamins. They are present in all the tissues of our body and are also in fluids. They maintain water balance in our body. They are helpful in clotting of blood and contraction of muscles. Calcium, magnesium, phosphorus, sodium, potassium are the five basic minerals for the body. Iron, copper, chromium, iodine, zinc and manganese are the trace elements.

We all know that calcium and phosphorus are required for healthy teeth and bones. Brain function depends on adequate magnesium, manganese, zinc and other essential minerals. Lack of iodine leads to goitre or thyroid. Minerals are also essential for regulation of osmotic pressure equilibrium. Minerals play a very important role in the complex processes going on in the body. Fruits, raw vegetables are rich source of minerals.

**Iron:-** Required by our body to make haemoglobin and myoglobin, both help carry and store oxygen in body.

**Phosphorus:-** It makes up 1% of our body weight and is present in each and every cell of our body. It is required for the formation for teeth and bones. It helps in synthesis of protein for cell repair.

**Manganese:-** It activates many important enzymes in the body which are crucial to amino acids and cholesterol. It is also required for the formation of cartilage and bone.

**Magnesium:-** It converts food into energy and regulates body temperature. It helps in absorption of calcium. It is very important for certain biochemical reactions including transmission of nerve impulses.

**Copper:-** It helps in absorption of iron in our body and regulating blood pressure. It is required for production of melanin a substance which gives colour to our hair and skin.

**Zinc:-** It is required by our body to make proteins and DNA. It builds our immune system and gives us sense of taste and smell.

**Selenium:-** We need this trace element in very small amount. But it is very essential in preventing cellar damage from free radicals. It also regulates thyroid functioning.

**Fibre:-** Nobody should even think of not having fibrous diet. Because you will start suffering from constipation if your body lacks fibre.

Dietary fibre or roughage is non-digestible component which is not absorbed by the body. It has important properties. It traps the water in our body and ensures that the waste matter does not dry up and cause constipation. It also throws the toxins out and reduces the risk of inflammation in intestines. Fibre also helps in lowering cholesterol level in our body. It also helps in reducing weight. There are many types of fibre water soluble and non soluble. Generally processed foods are devoid of fibres like rice. Insoluble fibres are found in vegetables with skin, whole grains, brown rice, cereal husk, esabgol etc . It helps in normal bowel functioning and thus in preventing constipation. It also lowers cholesterol.

Soluble fibre is available in oats, all fruits, vegetables and pulses. They are also helpful in reducing cholesterol in our body.

> *Medicinal vegetation and juices maketh Honey. Honey is like nectar. It is like the vital force. It is like cereals.' Hindu Scriptures.*

**Water:-** Also known as elixir of life. There is no life without water. It is not a nutrient but at the same time is very important for our body. Our Body needs lot of water to keep us healthy. Water has no calories, carbohydrates, proteins or fats; still we generally overlook it when we talk about nutrients.

1.  It lubricates our joints and keeps our body supple.

2.  It keeps our body temperature stable, cool in summers and warm in winters.

3.  It helps in excreting waste products from our body.

4.  It helps transport nutrients throughout the body.

5.  It also helps in digestion of food. Water helps in removing waste products from our body in the form of urine and sweat.

We lose water from our body as urine, perspiration and from lungs every day. We must drink enough of water daily. We take water in many forms such as food, fruits, vegetable, drinks juices, milk and tea etc. we should have more water during summers.

**Important Note:- We should not take too many medicines because there are certain medicines which take out certain Vitamins and minerals from our body. Vitamins are very helpful for the normal functioning of our system and fighting diseases. Here are names of certain medications which deplete our body of vitamins and minerals.**

| Medication | Vitamins and minerals |
|---|---|
| Antibiotics | Vitamin B and Vitamin K |
| Anti-inflammatory Drugs | Vitamin C, Folic acid and iron |
| Aspirin | Vitamin A, B, Calcium, iron, potassium and Folic acid |
| Caffeine | Vitamin B, Potassium and Zinc |
| Diuretics | Vitamin C, Zinc, Calcium, potassium and Iodine |
| Laxatives | Vitamin A,D,K and Potassium |
| Estrogens | Vitamin B6, Folic acid. |

## Alkaline and Acidic Balance in Food

Ramesh is working with multinational company. He does lot of travelling and partying. Naturally his drinking has also increase many folds . He started feeling pain in his joints , which with the time increased so much that finally he had to see a doctor. There he was told that inflammation in joints had started developing. It was in initial stage which could be cured by correcting his life style. As it was related to ph imbalance and accumulation of acid deposits in the joints it could harm cartilage. He was prescribed alkaline diet which consisted of lot of curds , ripe fruits ,sprouts , greens and salads. Specially alfa alfa sprouts. No drinking and change of life style completely.

Why it happened with Ramesh? Lets know about acid and alkali balance in our body.

In 1933, a New York doctor, William Howard Hay published a book 'A New Health Era, in which he said,' all disease is caused by autotoxication, due to acid accumulation in the body.' He further says that when the pH balance in our body starts suffering, a person becomes acidic, which means our body starts borrowing minerals (including calcium, sodium, potassium and magnesium) from vital organs and also bones to neutralize the acid. In the process it removes them from the body, thus weakening it.

It is not a new concept, centuries back Ayurveda believed that it is essential to balance the acid and alkali levels in our body to keep us healthy. Ayurveda has given many rules to balance these two factors.

## What is acid/alkaline imbalance?

Over-acidity leads to indigestion, and it depletes alkaline reserves in the body and makes us weakened. Healthy cells start dyeing prematurely.

The pH factor indicates acid/alkaline levels. This can vary from person to person. Experts have set a goal of a pH number of 7 for optimal health. So normal person should have a neutral pH of 7. If it is higher/low it can create problems. Any value under this indicates that you have acidity and values more than this indicate towards alkalinity. For example- pH value of Saliva is 6 and urine is 6.8 which show that they are towards more acidic in nature.

In fact to keep pH level balance we should consume 80% alkaline and 20% acidic food. Our body fluid such as blood, saliva, bile, urine all need alkaline level balanced to function well. Otherwise our kidneys, intestines, liver and lungs have to work harder.

pH balance is determined by the foods we eat. If we eat more of acidic food, we can be troubled by acidosis. Alternatively, if we are eating more of alkaline foods, our body could have too low of a pH. This condition is known as alkalosis.

## Disease of acidosis:-

Blood pressure, skin problems, constipation, cough, cold, premature ageing, low immunity, rheumatism etc. it slows down our metabolism and digestive system. One can develop neurological problems and bone loss.

Acidosis condition can be cured by diet which is alkaline. We should avoid acidic foods like sugars, Maida, coffee, chocolate, cakes eggs, meat etc. Rice, wheat, pulses all are acid –forming foods.

One should consume fresh vegetables, greens, salads, nuts and seeds which are alkaline forming foods. All fruits are alkaline. Citrus fruits are acidic in taste but during digestion they become alkaline. Foods that are rich in magnesium, potassium and sodium are alkaline. Also calcium rich food is alkaline in nature. All root vegetables and juices are alkaline.

## Diseases of alkalosis:-

Water retention, lethargy, sluggishness, lack of will power and concentration, multiple sclerosis, Parkinson. With negative thoughts and feelings alkalinity increases.

To cure this condition we should consume acidic food to keep the pH balance intact.

However, experts say that higher alkaline levels are less prone to health problems and have strong immune system.

Acidic/alkaline imbalance can create a vicious cycle that depletes energy, minerals and nutrients, and causes a multitude of potentially life-threatening conditions and diseases. It is high time we all should change and get into healthy food habits.

> *Carrot juice is a natural solvent for ulcerous and cancerous factors. It is a great lubricant and cleanser.*

## Prana in Food

Prana is the life force that sustains life of all living beings on this earth including plants, animals and human beings. In scientific terms it is called bioplasma and scientists measure its sphere of influence just like a force field. Besides oxygen food is the first and foremost thing that we need to be alive. Food not only gives us energy, it also gives us prana energy.

All vegetables, fruit and animal, have prana in it. That means before we plucked them , they had an independent existence and they were alive. Plant life produces food for itself in the form of starch and glucose which is the highest form of food that is directly synthesized anywhere in the world.

The prana energy in grain and produce depends on the conditions and circumstances under which they are grown. Also vegetables, wheat and fruits which we eat should be grown at a pollution free land and irrigated with pollution free water. Water should not be contaminated by chemicals and other pollutants. Land should not be spoilt by floods, droughts, too much heat or any other natural disaster. All these things spoil the cultivation. If there is any vitiation of prana in the atmosphere, crop grown here will also lack prana. The manner in which livestock such as chicks, fish and meat is kept also affects the prana energy in them. Such type of food consumed is not capable of giving prana energy to the person who consumes it. But we hardly have any control on these things.

But we do have control on certain other things such as mood of the cook, properly washing of the vegetables and eating food in calm environment with a happy mood etc. The person who cooks food should be in a happy mood while preparing food. Food should be prepared with love and care ,also has effect on the taste of the food . that is why food cooked by mothers tastes the best. These things are embedded in the Indian culture. **'Jaisa khao ann, vaisa ho munn' OR 'you are what you eat'** is a popular Indian saying.

A renowned French engineer has divided foods into four categories on the basis of electromagnetic waves that they emit. Scale is from o to 10,000 angstroms. This should match the basic scale of human wavelength which is 6.5000.

1St category:- Foods which emit vibrations or wavelength between 6.5000 to 10,000 angstroms are the best. These foods are fruits, fresh vegetables, whole grains, olive oil, ocean fish and shellfish.

2nd category:- Foods which have radiations between 6.5000 to 3000 angstroms are second best. These foods are peanut oil, boiled vegetables, eggs, sugar and cooked fish.

3rd category:-After this the radiations become weaker and level also goes down. Food with radiations below 3000 angstroms falls in third category. They are cooked meats, tea, coffee, chocolate, jams, all kinds of pickles, cheese. This includes all refined food, bleached food, polished food and refined oils including margarine. The last, fourth category has no prana in it.

# CHAPTER 4

# Theory of Food's Healing Powers

> 'Natural forces within us are the true healers of disease.'
>
> *- Hippocrates*

When Mukesh suffered from cancer of upper digestive track, his whole family was under shock and pain. Mukesh does not chew pan, tobacco, he does not smoke, still he suffered from cancer. He does not have any history of cancer. Though he has recovered now , but along with the medication he has to follow strict diet regimen.

Naina is diagnosed with heart problem, she has erratic food habits.

Geeta is balding inspite of taking good care of her hair . She is running from one doctor to the other one.

If I ask you ,'' What is common among heart diseases, cancers,, balding diabetes, arthritis, cerebrovascular disease, cataracts, aging , what will you say? Don't they sound different diseases? You will be surprised to know that they all share a common link which is called ' FREE RADICALS.'

Japanese biochemist Yukie Niwa, who is one of the most experienced free -radical researchers says ,' damaged free radicals are cause of upto 85% chronic and degenerative diseases.' According to some new researches Parkinson's and Alzheimer's are also attributed to free radicals. It damages our IMMUNE system.

If you have heard about somebody suffering from Parkinson's or diabetes , you must know that one of the reasons was damage to free radicals. Now you may ask me what are free radicals. Never mind , you are not the only one , 80% of the population does not know about it , even the people suffering from it. Even Mukesh also heard about free radicals when doctor told him that his cancer is caused by low immunity level and free radicals along with other factors.

Do not get perturbed if many people around you are talking about free radicals .The truth is free radicals do not harm us always. They are produced by our body because our body requires them for metabolic processes like digestion of food and converting it into energy. Our immune system produces free radicals which help in destroying viruses and bacteria. They also produce vital hormones. If our immune system is good and we are healthy, our body can keep a check on free radicals. But when they are produced in more quantity than required, they start harming us. They can destroy our body cells structure so badly that it affects our immunity and can alter DNA codes which are first step towards cancer.

First get to know what they actually are and what are the sources of them.

# What is a free radical?

Our bodies are composed of molecules which are made up of atoms like all matter in this world. Each atom has a nucleus and electrons which spin around it in an orbit. Electrons are always in balanced pair and it keeps molecule and atom stable. When a molecule loses one of its electrons it becomes unstable. This type of molecule is called 'Free Radical'. This kind of molecule is not able to give us energy. To be stable again it takes an electron from some other healthy molecule and damages that molecule. That molecule steals a molecule from another healthy molecule and damages yet another molecule and this chain process goes on and keeps damaging our healthy cells.

We all have heard that story of rotten onion in a basket, how one rotten onion spoils the other one and this one will spoil next one in line and they spoil the whole basket of onions. But onions are not lying in the body ,you can always pick up and through the rotten one. In this case we can't pick and choose the rotten free radical.

*Do not apply vitamin oils such as vitamin E capsules on your skin as our skin cannot absorb these oils. You have to eat them through food. That is the best way.*

## Sources of Free Radicals

Free radicals are formed in two ways -internal and external. We all know and have read in our class five science books that  when iron comes in contact with water and air, it starts rusting . While cooking when you cut brinjal or potato and leave it exposed to air , it turn brown, it happens because of oxidation. Same way oxidation happening in our body creates free radicals in fat, blood and tissue which is harmful. Superoxide, hydroxyl and lipid peroxide, singlet oxygen and hydrogen peroxide all these big names are free radicals and toxic forms of oxygen. They are formed through metabolic processes like digestion and respiration when the body is eliminating toxins out of body.

Our body converts food into energy with the help of oxygen. While doing this ,damaged oxygen molecule is left which is free radical. Also it uses some oxidants to fight bacteria, parasites and chronic infections. In the process other healthy cells are also exposed to free radicals.

*There are external sources also such as pesticides in food, stress in life, smoke, chemicals which make us venerable to free radicals.*

- Our body constantly produces free radicals every day.

- When our body is exposed to ultra violet rays from sun, gamma rays and x-rays from radioactive material , it produces large amount of free radicals.

- Animal fat, vegetables oils, fish oil and iron etc all can stimulate the formation of free radicals. We all know that animal fat is very harmful at the same time even vegetable fat is also harmful, but may not be to that extent. It is not bad for cholesterol but it does form free radicals. We should eat it in less quantity.

- The food which contains chemicals, pesticides, toxins, contaminated water, aerated drinks, junk food like pizza, burger, meat etc, smoking, drugs etc are all carriers of free radicals.

## Harm they do

1. They turn LDL cholesterol into a form which clogs arteries.

2. They can alter DNA codes which is the first step towards cancer.

3. They give problems of blood pressures, arthritis and asthma.

4. They can also damage sperm and cause infertility and birth related defects.

5. They can destroy eye cell and can cause eye related problem including macular degeneration.

6. They can cause neurological deterioration and related diseases.

7. They reduce our immunity by spoiling our immune system.

*Hence we see that in our everyday life we are constantly bombarded with free radical and cannot escape them.*

I do not want to scare you please.

God has given us natural way to get protected from free radicals. Our body produces enzymes that neutralize them. But we are faced by large amount of free radicals, and to neutralize such a big number, we need extra anti oxidants in our diet. Antioxidants are protective molecules also referred to as free radical scavengers.

Mukesh who was suffering from cancer, Geeta who was balding , Naina who had heart problem they all were told to take diet rich in antioxidants. Thousands others who suffer from other diseases such as diabetes, arthritis etc which we mentioned above need anti oxidants rich diet.

## Antioxidants:-

Our body cells have antioxidant system that neutralizes free radicals. Antioxidants, which we get from food, can protect us from the damage of free radicals. Antioxidants work by allowing themselves to be attacked and damaged by free radicals, sparing the cell itself. They are basically beta-carotene, vitamin C and E and selenium. Selenium is a trace element which is required for the proper functioning of anti oxidants enzyme systems.

## Beta-carotene

Plants have a vital chemical in their leaves called Beta-Carotene which they use to neutralize free radicals .Beta-Carotenes is also known as antioxidants because they block the tissue oxidation. When we eat fresh fruits and raw salads, we unknowingly are consuming Beta carotene and protecting ourselves against free radicals. Beta carotene is made up of two molecules of vitamin A. when beta carotene splits in our body, they yield its two molecules of vitamin A, which have some protective effect. It protects the skin against harsh sun rays and skin cancers.

> *When you keep water in bottles , it loses its life force.*
> *Water should be poured from one vessel to the other*
> *one for six to seven times before drinking and thus its*
> *life force should be reactivated. It also becomes tasty.*

Now you know that you don't have to go too far to get Beta-carotene . We can get it from green, yellow vegetables and fruits. We should include lot of vegetables and fruits in our diet. Some people depend upon the pills and capsules to get Beta carotene, but I would say that vegetable and fruits contain many other types of carotene and nutrients which help in the health of other body parts also . Many kinds of beta carotene which are called carotenoids are found in vegetables. Also if one kind of beta carotene is consumed in large amount may reduce absorption of other carotenoids. Vegetables and fruits are natural and balanced mix of all antioxidants. Next time your mom or someone keeps vegetables and fruits on your platter, I am sure you are not going to say no.

## Vitamin C, E and selenium:-

You knew that vitamin E and C are very good for your shining skin. Thats true. Along with it , this is also equally true that vitamin C is also very potent antioxidant which circulates in bloodstream and protects us from free radicals. Vitamin E which does not prevent the formation of free radicals but it does stop chain reaction of molecular damage. In cell membrane free radicals come in contact with vitamin E and damage them by altering them chemically. But Vitamin C repairs vitamin E and brings it in fighting form. Is it too much for you? Then here is simple table.

| Antioxidants | High amount | Normal amount |
|---|---|---|
| Beta-carotene | Sweet potato, spinach, liver, egg yolk , carrots, broccoli, pumpkin,grains. | Brussels sprouts, grape fruit, orange, milk, tomato, peaches |
| Vitamin-C | Orange, broccoli (also known as green cauliflower), Brussels, cauliflower, grapefruit, pineapple, strawberry, sweet potato. | Apple, corn kernel, carrots, soya beans, spinach |
| Vitamin -E | Soyabean, brown rice, navy beans, corn kernels, wheat, fish, seeds Brussels sprouts | Sweet potato , spinach, corn, nuts, chickpeas ,apricots. All oils |
| Selenium | Fish, brazil nuts and whole grains | |

## Note:-

1. Red grapes have more antioxidants than green or white grapes.

2. Olive oil is rich source of antioxidants.

3. Red and yellow onions are better than white ones.

4. Raw garlic which is also known as Jammu garlic is much better and is odourless in case you have an aversion.

**Beware of your iron:-** Yes, beware of your iron intake. As we know now that free radicals form because of oxidation. Iron carries oxygen in the blood but if our body has iron in excess it starts harming our body by catalyzing the formation of free radicals.

Dr Lauffer has said,' iron is a key component of the free radical theory of disease.'' Your body is a sort of dead end for iron.'

This means we can get rid off extra sodium in our body, but extra iron is impossible to throughout. It remains in our body to give problems. We should limit intake of iron and unnecessary taking iron pills should be avoided.

**Cholesterol:-**

**When Ashok got his blood test done, he came to know that his cholesterol was very high. He didn't believe and even his family members also couldn't believe it. He went to a different pathological lab for second opinion, but there was no change in the reports. Reports were telling the same story. Why Ashok could not believe was because he is very slim trim. He was advised certain diet and exercise and his cholesterol levels came down and now he is ok.**

Cholesterol by its name can scare anybody. What all high cholesterol can do we know it pretty well. It is regarded as one of the most important risk factors for developing heart disease. Anybody can suffer from high cholesterol whether he is fat or slim, young or old , male or female.

# Have you ever seen cholesterol?

Cholesterol is white, lacy, thick substance which looks like wax, found in most body tissues. our body has three types of fat- triglycerides , phospholipids and sterols. It is the main ingredient in the lining of the arteries. Our body makes sufficient amount of cholesterol for its own needs, we do not require it from other sources. In fact all animals have cholesterol in their body. Diet rich in animal fat gives us cholesterol as well as saturated fat but no antioxidant and fibre. If we take food which is high in fat , we are harming ourselves because it does not dissolve in blood. Fat particles get mixed with proteins and form into small particles called lipoproteins and then transported in the body.

Now lipoproteins are also of two types : LDL (Low Density Lipoproteins) and HDL(High Density Lipoproteins). LDL is also Called bad protein because it gets deposited in coronary and cerebral arteries. HDL is good cholesterol because it helps to remove the fat from body through the production of bile in the digestive tract.

we need cholesterol for Blood clotting, insulating nerve fibres, nourishing the brain and manufacture of sex hormones. cholesterol levels can vary from day to day by about 6 %. A little stress can cause variation.

If your cholesterol levels are high you should reduce intake of fat to reduce the cholesterol level. This we can do by eating diet which is low fat or fat free.

> *All the foods have healing and preventive powers. First they heal the body and they attack the disease. When the body becomes healthy it automatically fights the disease.*

**Menu:-**

Empty stomach you may have garlic with warm water.

Early morning (any of these things):- Apple, one small bowl papaya, banana, watermelon, pear, peach, chikoo.

Breakfast:- any cereal, roti or paratha( without oil, ghee) made of wheat / millet/ barley/soya/ ragi.

Mid-Morning:- buttermilk

Lunch:- Curd/Raita, vegetable, dal, chapati/brown rice. (you can change the grain from breakfast, no ghee or butter in dal, vegetable should be prepared in one table spoon of oil).

No water till one hour. And while eating you can take one or two sips, otherwise it will dilute your digestive juices.

Evening:- green tea (without sugar) /lime juice/ buttermilk. This time you can have flex seeds /almonds/ walnuts (only a few)

Dinner :- only green vegetable, salad.

Eat dinner around 7:30/8:00 PM two hours before going to bed.

When you prepare dal add onion, garlic, ginger, tomato at the time of cooking, it will be tasty. Add spices to your own taste. Eat lot of fiber so that you are not constipated.

Shun all fried stuff and oily stuff. No refined flour. No white rice.

Along with it walk and cardio exercises is must. Once your cholesterol goes down you can add a few more things ( non oily) according to your taste. If you feel that you are still hungry have a chapati also at night.

## Fats :-

Indian food , basically contains lot of fat all over India. North Indian food like butter chicken, daal makhani, parathas, bhindi fry etc, khakras, chile, mathari, bengali sweets in abundance, alu in every fried form, down south dosas are fried and lot of coconut preparations all this is very oily. On top of this fried snacks from all over are available now all over India. We have to be very careful in preparing food.

> We get fat from our daily seeds, vegetables and wheat. Mustard oils is from mustard, wheat germ oil is from wheat, corn oil is from corn. Fish oil from fish. So whatever oil you are using for cooking is extra . Now you may guess about frying , cakes and fancy salads.

Here we will not talk much about the types of fat as we have already discussed in detail about it in previous chapter. It is recommended to avoid taking saturated fats which are always in solid form. Whereas unsaturated fats are in liquid from. Though they are still ok. **But unsaturated fats have their own problems because they increase formation of free radicals and tend to impair immune system.** So if you see fat is not good for us . But liquid oils are still ok. And we must use them in minimum quantity.

**Saturated fatty oils:-** palm oil, coconut oil, palm kernel oil, margarine, all hydrogenated oils( vegetable oils are chemically solidified into saturated fats.

**Unsaturated fatty oils:-** safflower oil, sunflower oil, canola oil, corn oil, olive oil, peanut oil, sesame oil, soya bean oil.

When your body has too much fat , it gets oxidized and turns rancid and produces free radicals which damage our cells. They attack our system daily because we keep on consuming foods rich in cholesterol such as pizzas, burgers, sweets, cakes, cheese, meat etc. They attack our brain cells. It not only results in weight gain but it also makes us prone to diseases like diabetes, cancer, heart problems etc.

Fats which are in their natural state are not bad for us. Fat in nuts like almonds, pistachio, walnuts, and flaxseeds is good for us, but only in moderation.

> *Fat should not be over heated. Deep frying which is overheating leads to the formation of dangerous peroxides which are very harmful for our body.*

Refined oils are very risky for us. While refining oils , vital nutrients in oil are damaged and free radicals are formed.

1. If you are eating any meat, remove extra visible fat before cooking. My suggestion is avoid meat and eat fish instead.

2. Use lot of green vegetables , in fact all of them, in all possible colours. Each colour gives you some or the other benefit. Tomato, brinjal, pumpkin, spinach, methi, caulifloer, bittergaurd, bottlegaurd, lady finger whatever is available.

3. Drumsticks are full of vitamins. Chestnut has amazing benefits. Coconut water.

4. Eat all seeds, they all contains natural oils.

5. All pulses contain natural oils.

6. Do not leave nuts almonds, walnuts, brazil nuts, cashew(in limited quantity), peanuts.

7. All fruits including dates and figs.

Nature has given us so much and in such a large variety but we run after junk food.

**Wonder Vitamin**

**Frankly speaking I didn't know about OPC. Its by chance that I came to know about it. I was sitting with one of my doctor friends and she mentioned about it. Then I did research about it**

**OPC: The Multifunctional Antioxidant**

After decades of research, OPC has been given the official recognition and distinction as "vitamin P. "Full form of OPC is oligomeric proanthocyanidins and it is one of the most powerful antioxidant free radical scavengers. Also known as 'youth nutrient', OPC supports functions of Vitamin C in the body. Some of the antioxidants increase potential of other antioxidants and some other ones can regenerate more and other antioxidants. OPC is such a antioxidant that protects vitamin C, thus delivering more vitamin C to the cells for nourishment. It is capable in protecting the brain and central nervous system. Grape seed has OPC in abundance. OPC is non-toxic and strengthens capillaries and arteries. It supports memory retention, reduces stress, and helps to maintain joint flexibility. It is also known to improve skin texture and maintains proper circulation.

# CHAPTER 5
# Nature's 'bowl'

> 'Food alone is the best medicine for all living creatures because they have come into existence because of the food alone' -
>
> - *Taitriya Upanished*

My nephew kairon ( 10 years old) was a non-vegetarian and relished his meals which consisted only meat, chicken , fish , prawns, pork etc. ( he stayed abroad till he was 8 years old). We all used to tell him to eat fruit , chapati, pulses etc. but he never listened. For him bread and non-vegetarian food was the only thing to eat in this world. He started developing cracks in his tongue. We took him to many doctors but no relief. Then one day someone told us about an ayurvedic doctor . We took the child to him. He told us that he should stop eating non-vegetarian food immediately and start eating fresh vegetables and pulses . but the child refused to eat all vegetarian food. Then we slowly started giving him green vegetables and pulses. It took him more than 6 months to get fully cured.

Nature has given us bounty full fresh eats, we must make full use of them.

# 1. Grains and pulses.

**Wheat, rice, barley, rye, oats (Jowar), bajra, corn, flax, buckwheat, sorghum, quinoa :**

Grains are unprocessed form of seeds, their bran or germ has not been removed. There is also processed form or refined form such as bread, cake, pastries, refined flour, refined rice etc. Grains are eaten either as whole grains or in powder/ flour form. Grains can also be eaten in roasted, beaten, soaked, sprout, boiled or cooked form. Oats is beaten form of oat grain which we have with milk in the form of porridge. Popcorn is roasted form of corn grain. Indian chapatti or brown bread is baked form. Kheer (one type of sweet dish) is cooked form of rice grain. Whole grains are more nutritious than its refined form.

Whole grains contain some valuable antioxidants which are not found in vegetables and fruits. They contain photochemical, proteins, thiamine etc in large amount. They are full of fibre, selenium, magnesium and potassium. Whole grains can also lower our low-density lipoprotein (LDL) cholesterol, insulin levels and triglycerides and save us from cardiovascular diseases. They are helpful in reducing the risk of diabetes, obesity, constipation, cancer. Whole grains also lower cholesterol levels in our body.

We must take brown rice, wheat with bran, shredded wheat and shredded oats, flaks of grains, roasted wheat, bajra and jowar. Insoluble fibre which we get from wheat, brown rice, barley, corn increase the content of fibre in our body. So that problem of constipation remains at bay. Whole grains have laxative effect on the bowels. Oat and flax are soluble fiber which fill with water and take the shape of jelly like structure. Then they easily pass through the colon and keep our digestive system healthy. Refined flour which has little nutrition sticks to our intestine and gets rotten, it makes our intestines weak and hinders our bowel moment.

---

1. *Whole grains should be soaked in water for some time and then washed properly so that any chemicals, germs or insecticides are also removed.*

2. *To reduce cooking time for grains soak them for a few hours or overnight.*

---

## Legumes or Lentils / Pulses.

Also known as lentils legumes include all types of beans( kidney beans, broad beans, white beans, black one eyed beans), dry peas, chickpeas , mung , masoor, arhar, urad ( whole and split).

Lentils are rich source of proteins, vitamin B group, low glycemin(DI), carbohydrates, dietary fibre, minerals and fiber. At the same time they are free of saturated fats and have no cholesterol (except soya beans and peanuts). They also have phytonutrients such as isoflavones and lignans.

Research has shown that lentils can prevent chronic diseases such as diabetes, overweight cardiovascular disease and also keep the stomach healthy. People whose intake of legumes is higher have higher longevity. High resistant starch content in lentils is healthy for the colon because it is fermented by colonic bacteria to short chain fatty acids. They are low in saturated fat and hence keep us healthy.

Lentils are low in amino acid methionine where as grains are high in this substance. On the other hand lentils are rich source of essential amino acid lysine and grains contain low level of this substance. It is always advisable to mix both in your diet to gain maximum advantage of both. In India we combine lentils with rice and chapatti; in other countries they consume tofu with rice and tortilla (corn) with beans.

Some lentils do not suit everybody. They cause bloating and gas after eating. But in India we mix lot of spices, garlic, ginger and onion to cut this effect. Also if we take them in germination form (sprout) or fermentation form (with probity's) we can get large benefits and also the gastric and bloating effect will be reduced.

## 2. Vegetables and fruits

Dark green leafy vegetables provide us concentrated form of nutrition. They are naturally very low in calories and fat and do not have cholesterol at all. We must eat vegetables in one of our meals every day. Vegetables are a rich source of vitamins including K,C,E,B (B1 and B2),minerals like iron, calcium, potassium, phytonutrients like beta-carotene, lutein and also omega-3 fatty acids. Vitamins and calcium is beneficial for reproductive health and menopause. They protect our cells from damage. Vitamin K which is found in abundance in leafy greens had many benefits for us. It regulates blood clotting, protects us from inflammatory diseases like arthritis, it also reduces atherosclerosis by reducing calcium in arterial plaques. It is a fat-soluble vitamin so we can cook green leafy vegetables with a little of oil.

Green vegetables contain carbohydrate in minimal quantity and they have very little impact on blood glucose. Vegetables contain lot of water and nutritious juices which hydrate our body and replenish liquid in the system. We get lot of fiber from the vegetables which regulate our bowels and keep our colon healthy. They thus protect us from many chronic diseases like constipation etc. fiber also is helpful in reducing the cholesterol level and thus reducing the risk of heart disease.

Energy which we get from green vegetables contains lot of prana which is good for body, mind and soul.

Vegetables are full of antioxidants which prevent aging. Potassium in fruits and vegetables reduces the risk of kidney stones and helps in lowering bone loss. It is also good to maintain blood pressure.

> *Tomato is good for health. It is used raw as well as in cooking. But its nutrition value increases many fold during cooking.*

## Fruits :-

We should eat fruits in raw and ripe stage. In western countries they make many kinds of sweet dishes by cooking fruits such as apple pie, fruit crumble, mango mousse etc. But raw fruits are better than cooked or processed ones. Raw fruits are full of enzymes and nutrients. In cooking they lose their nutrients. We get vitamins, minerals, thiamine, and other antioxidants from fruits, and many nutrients which are missing in vegetables are also found in fruits. They are easy to digest and because of the bulk have cleansing effect on intestines and bowls. They contains good amount of water content and very less amount of fat and proteins. They are highly alkaline.

Fruits make a good combination with milk and not with meals. Early morning is the best time to eat fruits. If one wants to have fruit juice, it should be consumed immediately otherwise it starts decomposing. Orange and mousami juices turns sour and harmful.

## 3. Nuts and seeds:-

Sunflower, pumpkin, almonds, peanuts, Brazil nuts, soya, alfalfa, cashew, walnut, and pistachio all come under the category of seeds and nuts. They are high in proteins and unsaturated fatty acids which are good for health. They contain many types of vitamins, antioxidants, zinc and lecithin also. Nuts and seeds also contain pectin and phytates . They also eliminate toxins from the body and thus reduce the level of free radicals. Nuts like Walnuts, hazelnuts etc and seeds like sesame seeds, pumpkin and sunflower seeds are rich source of vitamins.

Best vitamin which also prevents premature aging is Vitamin C, is found in plenty in seeds. All seeds after sprouting contain vitamin C and A in high amount. All nuts are eaten raw. Almonds can be soaked overnight for better results. We should not fry dry fruits and seeds. We can roast them.

## 4. Herbs and spices :-

In Asian countries herbs, spices and condiments are used in large amount. Herbs have antioxidant properties and they help reducing free radicals from the body. They also detoxify and strengthen our immune system. Tulsi, mint, green coriander, celery, ajwain, dill (soya), parsley, thyme all are very good for our health.

Spices and condiments are useful in abdominal cramps, constipation, gas, flatulence, gout, headache, respiratory disorders, toothache etc. some have antiseptic qualities like turmeric. Almost all the spices have medicinal value. . Today turmeric is known as prevention of cancer all over the world. Fenugreek is useful for gout and diabetes. Fennel is useful to relieve flatulence. Chillies are good in vitamin c. Ajwain is good in stomach pains.

## 5. Fish:-

In many populations fish is treated as vegetable from the sea. In west Bengal they call it jaltori. Seafood are very rich source of minerals, potassium, Zinc, magnesium and trace elements. Thus they are potent to fight against free radicals. Fish is full of omega-3 fatty acids (unsaturated fats) which are good for the health of our heart. They reduce the risk of dying from heart disease. It also lowers the cholesterol levels in our blood. Omega-3 is responsible in reducing inflammation in our body which can damage our blood vessels and eventually lead to heart problems.

Research has shown that they may prevent macular degeneration, a form of blindness, has positive influence on rheumatoid arthritis, asthma and kidney disease. They also decrease triglycerides, boost immunity and reduce blood clotting.

Salmon, trout, tuna, herring are rich source of omega-3 fatty acids. Whereas tilapia and catfish are high in unhealthy fatty acids. Fish taken in boiled or baked form is the healthiest. Open water fish is always better than farm produced fish which can be harmful because it may contain pesticides or other chemicals used in raising farmed fish. Do not overeat fish. Fish should be eaten twice a week to get benefits from them.

> Pumpkin is very good for strengthening the cell structure because it contains chlorophyll, minerals and amino acids which produce the red pigment of blood cells.

## CHAPTER 6
# Truth about oils

'Never use leftover fried oil as it contains terrible toxins. Cooked oil turns rancid very fast. It contains some chemicals which are harmful for us'

Some guests arrived at Harpreet's place without informing her. She didn't panic at all. She had kept a karahi in one corner of her kitchen with oil in it. This was used oil ( she had used it for frying pakoras three days back ) which she was going to reuse for frying. She used it for frying pakoras. She picked up another karahi with some used oil and added some extra oil and fried chicken kababs in it. She turned towards me ,' See, how simple it is. I keep everything ready. I never have any problem when some guests arrive uninformed. Karahi chadao , take out half fried stuff from the freezer , fry it and serve.' I had a heart to tell her that it is not that simple , what all these reused oils do with our health , we come to know only later on. By adding fresh oil in used oil she spoiled the fresh oil also. Like Harpreet there are N number of people who reuse the oil. All restaurants , dhabas and hotels do this. Some people know about it and some may not be knowing.

## Truth about oils:-

All types of oils are good whether it is olive oil, or

mustard, sesame, rapeseed, walnut and canola. We must consume a variety of oils because each has different properties and benefits for us. By using all types of oils we will be able to take balanced omega-3 and omega-6 fatty acids. Both are essential for our body. Natural fats which we get from milk and milk products are not really harmful but synthetic fats are really bad and harmful for us.

How we cook food creates the entire problem. Cooking done at very high temperature such as frying etc destroys many of the nutrients and it also turns the oil carcinogenic. Must check what is written on the oil can, check its smoke point. If it is high then the oil is good for frying. If it is low then best is to use it for salads etc. If the smoke point of the oils is above 210 degree Celsius it comes under high smoke point category, if it is less than 177 degree Celsius it falls under low category. It should not be cooked at all. Otherwise it will harm us.

There was a time when only a limited variety of oils was available in the market. Now with the western culture prevailing , and multinationals coming to India, a large variety of oils are available . one can choose accordingly.

> *You should use very little oil for cooking. You can use an aerosol spray for pouring oil for cooking. This is a good way for limiting and pouring exact amount of oil.*

**Avocado oil:** It has a higher smoking point than all plant oils, it is good to used for frying .It is a good source of vitamin E. It's lovely flavour makes it ideal for dressings. It also contains lutein, an antioxidant which is good for eye health. It's expensive oil but nothing is expensive to get good health..

**Canola oil:** It has a high smoke point, so it is ideal for cooking. This oil has very low levels of saturated fat . it has more heart-friendly omega-3 than olive oil.

**Flaxseed oil:** Made from the seeds of the flax plant, this oil contains high levels of omega-3 and omega-6 fatty acids. It has a very low smoke point, so it should not be used for cooking but is good for salads.

**Grape seed oil:** this oil has a high smoking point, so it can be used for cooking. Though it lacks antioxidants but is a good source of both vitamin E and oleic acid which reduces the risk of heart problems.

**Hemp oil:** hemp oil has low smoke point hence should not be used for cooking. It is green colour oil because it contains high chlorophyll content. It is a rich source of both omega-3 and omega-6 fatty acids. It also contains gamma linolenic acid (GLA) which helps in maintaining healthy cholesterol and blood pressure levels. Hemp oil keeps the hormonal levels balanced.

*You can store oil in refrigerator or in a cool, dark place if your kitchen remains hot during summers. As it heat can damage it. Oil may turn cloudy in fridge but its quality will remain safe and the cloudiness will also disappear when you keep the oil out for some time.*

**Mustard oil:** this is very good oil with a high smoke point which makes it excellent for even frying. Study by the All India Institute of Medical Sciences, New Delhi found that mustard oil is high in Mufa and Puf Extra virgin olive oil, for example, has a low smoke point, so if you use it to cook something like a stir-fry where you need the oil to be really hot, you will not only lose the benefits of olive oil, it will also cause harm. It has both omega-6 and omega-3.

**Olive oil:** Extra virgin olive oil has a low smoke point, so if you use it for cooking it will be harmful. Avoid for deep frying and cooking food. Expensive on pocket and bad for cooking . so you will lose the benefits of olive oil.

> *Oils with high omega-3 content (i.e.: hempseed oil, flax oil, walnut oil) are not suitable for cooking. They can be used in salads.*

**Rapeseed oil:** The taste of rapeseed oil is neutral. It has a high smoke point, so can be safely used for cooking. it has one of the lowest contents of saturated fat among oils. It is a good source of both Mufa and Pufa.

**Walnut oil:** It has a high smoke point, so is good for cooking. It is a rich source of alpha-linolenic acid (ALA). Plant-based ALA is known to lower the risk of type 2 diabetes. It has a very nice flavour , which makes it good for salad dressings.

**Saffola, sunflower, groundnut oil:** All are widely used for cooking. Oils should be used in less quantity. The oil which has been used once for frying should not be reused as it becomes harmful. Omega-3 and omega -6 should be used in equal amounts in our diet. Most of the diets lack omega-3 hence we should try and use both in equal amount. Excess of omega-6 is not good as it can promote heart problems, even cancer and, reduce immunity. We must use oils rich in omega-3 .

Note- You should restrict your intake of omega-6 fatty acids such as sunflower seed oil, safflower oil and corn oil.

I must tell you what Gunita has been doing. She uses oil free or low fat snacks and feels proud of it. She cooks her food in low fat butter ( ?), takes oil free biscuits along with her morning and evening tea. Eat low fat chips and the list is endless. Not one or two, but four biscuits at one time. Once when she served low fat snacks to her friends, they were a little reluctant to eat. she insisted,' Are, its low fat. Nothing is going to happen. Have it.' I was watching all this drama. All this low fat stuff has some amount of fat in it and this is that trans fat which is very bad for our health. They clog our arteries. Do not fall into this trap. Just touch and see these low fat chips or snacks or biscuits, do you see something shining on your finger tip? Yes? This is oils. The lesson you learnt is' nothing is low fat'

*Drinking luke warm water flushed out extra oil from the body. Also it is good for the throat, after consuming oily food.*

 # CHAPTER 7

# Part - 2

> 'Immunity is the power to defend our body against any disease and also the power to fight the progress of the disease.'
>
> **_Ayurveda_**

## Boost your immunity

Every change of season Rajan used to be down with viral and it always took him at least 7-8 days to get cured. After that it was recovery period because viral really drains out a person completely. He was missing his school at least one and a half month during the year. Initially his Mom thought that it was seasonal viral and but on recurring illness she also got worried and alarmed . This time she was really tense about his health . Doctors told his mother that his immunity had gone very low. He was prescribed certain diet , exercises and medication to build immunity. He is a chubby child and you cann't make out that Rajan can have bad health. He used to thrive on junk food, Maggie noodles, aerated drinks a lot. Rajan is not the only child , nowadays even grownups are also seen getting affected by low immunity which creates havoc in their life.

My grandmother used to say if your immune system is 'Tagda'( strong in English) then you too are tagda. To have a strong immune system our diet should be good. A strong immune system can keep away all the diseases. This is a well known fact that food contains all the nutrients which are required to keep our system strong, healthy and fit.

## Why our immunity goes down:-

Stress of today's multitasking life is one of the major factors which has reduced our immunity. Food what we eat is full of additives , pesticides and chemicals. Water which we drink is contaminated. Even the air we breathe in is also polluted. Eating out day and night adds to the woes. All this is affecting our immunity and reducing white blood corpuscles (WBC), the real frontline warriors of our body. White blood cells of our body kill the bacteria, infection and cancerous cells. Thus saves us from various diseases. To make our system strong, we should go for natural foods which act to stimulate the immune system and make it stronger. If we take care of our diet, we need not depend on medicines for boosting our immunity.

## Immunity boosting foods

**Garlic:-** I have seen and known people who take garlic regularly in the morning, their cholesterol level never goes more than 150. Garlic is good in many ways. It lowers the cholesterol levels in body, fights bacteria , viruses and cancer. Garlic stimulates the potency of T-lymphocytes and macrophages which play important part in immunity related functions. Garlic should be consumed empty stomach early morning.

**Shiitake Mushrooms:-** Chinese have been knowing

about the healing powers of shiitake mushrooms since ancient times. They have been in use as medicinal mushrooms in Japan, Vietnam, Korea and Thailand. Also known as black mushrooms , they contain an antiviral substance called lentinan that has antitumor, cholesterol-lowering and immune stimulating properties. Lentinan is also known to boost functioning of macrophages and T-lymphocytes. They produce interferon, a kind of natural protein that stop multiplying of the viruses. There is another component, known as 1,3-beta glucan, which reduces tumour growth and reduces the side effects of cancer treatment. As a medicine, the extracts of compounds in shiitake mushrooms are recommended, not the mushroom itself. In Japan lentinan is given to cancer patients along with chemotherapy. Lentinan can also modify cells to resist the spreading of lung cancer cells. Activated hexose-containing compound is sold as a nutritional supplement in the United States, Europe, and Japan.

> *Shiitake mushrooms produce interferon, a kind of natural protein that stop multiplying of the viruses.*

**Zinc:-** zinc is one food which is very essential for a good immune system. It is said that zinc may restore declining immune system which happens after the age of 60. After a certain age our thymus gland , responsible for immune defences starts shrinking. A regular dose of zinc helps in restoring the health of thymus gland.

**Vitamin E:-** This wonder Vitamin is very potent in antioxidants which act like a protective shield guarding against any attack on lipids. It also boosts immunity. It does not let the fat oxidized by free radicals because it is rich in antioxidants. We get lot of vitamin E from groundnuts, seeds, almonds, corn. Wheat germ, coconut, and soybeans. Cold pressed vegetables oils such as sunflower also contain Vitamin E.

**Vegetables and Fruits:-** Many vegetables and fruits which are rich in Beta carotene and vitamin A and C also boost our immune system. Sweet potato, spinach, pumpkin, carrots, tomato, beetroot are all rich in beta carotene. Carotene also works against bacterial and viral infections. If taken around 30-50-mg of beta carotene regularly, it improves our immunity to great extent. One study says that vegetarians have more powerful white blood cells than non -vegetarians. Plant foods contain many such compounds which help boosting immunity.

> Fruits , natures gift , elixir of life are high in antioxidants, vitamins, and other nutrients.

## Vigour , Vitality and energy :-

How much energy we have, depends upon what goes in our stomach. If we are eating food which is oily, refined, full of starch, junk food, with no nutrients, tinned or canned food, surely we are not getting any benefits from it. Hence our energy level will also deplete. If it carries on for a long time it leads to ailments. Fresh food which is full of PRANA also contains lot of vitamins and nutrient .This nutrient rich food should be eaten properly, digested properly and eaten in less amounts, eaten at right time then only our digestive system can turn it into energy. There are certain ways to get maximum energy from the food we eat. Avoid any kind of junk food. Drink enough of water and juices so that it clears the kidneys and rehydrates our body cells. Sleep well. When you get up in the morning you should feel fresh. Avoid any kind of mental stress. Digest food properly.

# Sharpen your Intellect

My grandmother used to soak almonds in a cup of water at night and early morning she used to peel it and all of us used to eat it. 11 badams per person, that was the dose. After her, I saw my mother doing it. And now I do it for my children. In Indian homes such things become tradition. Nobody questions why we eat almonds this way, but 80% Indian surely are eating almonds this way. They say almonds are very good for the brain. If you soak it at night and eat in the morning, its heat generating properties die. Even the research done also authenticate this truth.

Food has tremendous effect on human body including brain and other parts. New researches in this field reveal that what you eat can make you intelligent, active, thinker, aggressive depressed and alert. Food deficient in certain nutrients can really play havoc with our brain waves and functioning. Dr Richard Wurtman is the man who takes the credit of discovering the effects of food on the activities of our brain. First eight years of a child's life are very crucial when he learns and develops behavior patterns at a fast pace. Blood vessels in brain require lot of oxygen for healthy functioning. Brain needs energy in large amount to process and store information .For this it needs oxygen, glucose and other nutrients. Lack of nutrients' supply to brains leads to short term memory loss and mental dullness. Also if it does not get nutrients and oxygen in proper amount and regularly, signs of lethargy, dizziness etc start showing. Foods that generate gas in stomach also make a person giddy.

Also we lose some of the memory with age but we can keep check on this to some extent. We should exercise our brain by using it. Along with it we should consume all the vital nutrients necessary for the brain to function actively. If we really want our food to empower our brain, mental alertness, to strengthen our memory and increase our concentration, there should be regular supply of oxygen to brain. Ample amount of nutrient should be consumed to allow the synthesis and release of neurotransmitters. Neurons in brains require oxygen and nutrients and the removal of free radicals which cause hindrance in the functioning of neurons.

Glucose level in our body should be balanced, level which is too low shows symptoms of confused thinking, and too high level damages cells in our brain and entire body. ( Salk institute for biological studies in California).

> *Cow's colostrum ( milk given by a cow within 8 hours of the birth of its calf) is high in anti-ageing properties.*

**Sharpen your brain:-** B Vitamins (thiamin ( B1 ),niacin(B3), vitamin B12 and B6) ,ribofin. Carotene, iron, citrus fruits, omega-3 fatty acids, Indian Brahmi, Chinese ginseng, certain fruits and vegetables all are very effective for the sound development of brain.

Research have shown that vitamin B family( particularly water soluble ones) has great effect on brain functioning. They help in converting glucose into energy.

**Vitamin B 1(Thiamin):-** low levels of thiamin, also called nerve vitamin, are linked to impairment in brain activity. We get this vitamin from wheat germ, nuts, cereals, bran and meat.

**Vitamin B3(niacin):-** vital for the red blood cells to carry oxygen effectively. A disease known as pellagra is caused by severe deficiency of niacin.

**Vitamin B6:-** Deficiency can cause slow learning and visual disturbances.

**Vitamin B12:-** Deficiency of this vitamin can cause depression at old age, nerve dysfunction and impaired mental activity. Plays an important role in the formation of myelin sheath around nerve fibres.

**Ribofin:-** Very good for boosting memory. We can get Ribofin from milk, almonds, and fortified cereals.

**Carotene : -** Very good for brains health. We can get it from citrus fruits and carrots.

**Iron:-** Research has shown that when adequate amount of iron was given to older people, they showed same type of EEG brain-wave activity as found in young adults.

**Folic acid:-** We need it for DNA synthesis. It is vital for the development of foetal nervous system.

**Fruits:-** fruits and nuts, high in boron, a trace element affect the electrical activity of brain positively. According to psychologist James Pen land (US-department of agriculture's grand fork human nutritional research center, deficiency of boron produces more theta waves and fewer alpha waves, which happens when we are sluggish. Our brain starts working slow. Bilberry taste sour and cooling. They are very high in antioxidants. They are beneficial for brain aging and neurological disorders. Bilberry extract strengthens the blood-brain barrier by acting on collagen fibers to protect sensitive peptide bonds from attack. It improves the weakness of nervous system. For serious diseases such as macular degeneration, we need bilberry extract in concentrated form. Apple contains quercetin which protects against memory loss. Grapes are rich source of quercetin and anthocyanin which again protects against memory loss.

**Fish:-** fish is high in protein, vitamins, minerals and many other trace elements from fish such as phosphorus and iodine which are vital for growth hormones. Its high quality protein is easily digestible. Essential amino acids present in it are more in comparison to vegetables.

Zinc is very important for brain health and we can get lot of it from sea food. Besides nutrients, It also gives us omega 3 polyunsaturated fatty acids. Omega 3 play very important role in making the blood less sticky and hence preventing the formation of clots in brain or any other part of the body. Because clot can travel from any part of the body to brain in no time and cause brain stroke. Omega 3 fatty acids are also helpful for people who suffer from hypertension. They require a small amount of it.

Fish oil obtained from fatty fish is the richest source of oil that is vital to normal brain development in unborn babies and infants. Thus it makes fish a vital food for pregnant women.

Study was conducted by UCLA researchers ( medical journal of American Academy of Neurology), according to that a diet lacking in omega-3 fatty acids may cause your brain to age faster and lose some of its memory and thinking capabilities.

**Herbs for Brain:-** there are certain herbs which are helpful in improving blood flow to brain, transportation of oxygen and nutrient to brain. It also improves cellular health and memory. There 4 herbs which together are called 4 Gs. Gotu kola, Siberian ginseng, panax ginseng and gingko biloba. They are helpful in improving alertness, concentration and intelligence. Gotu kola improves circulation, improving brain performance and memory. Gingko biloba boosts memory by improving blood circulation. Some of the herbs such as Calaguala and samambaiac are used to treat dementia and Alzheimer's disease. Rosemary, brahmi improve brain activity and performance. Research shows that these herbs protect against brain cells degeneration. Peppermint and yerba mate improve brain function.

**Tea:-** About 5000 years ago Chinese emperor Shen Nung discovered a wild leaf which on boiling in hot water produced a beverage and he named it 'cha', which is today's chai or tea. Tea contains a calming amino acid called thiamine which keeps our mind relaxed and enhanced concentration.It is a rich source of antioxidants called polyphenols and caffeine. According to a study the University of Limburg in the Netherlands caffeine is useful in the improvement of higher cognitive functions. Polyphones also help in improving cognitive function and memory.

### Food Habits: -

1. Eat more frequent but smaller meals.( 25 grams of glucose in blood at a time) to increase brain power.

2. Eat lower on glycemic index. (GI) eat foods that do not raise your blood sugar instantly. Carrots are low on GI. White bread is high in GI index.

3. Fat intake should be low in your diet. I say low, not zero fat.

4. Less food and more exercise is also not recommended.

> Our brain weighs 2% of the entire body weight but consumes roughly 20% of our daily calories.

## Elevate your mood

There is no doubt in the fact that certain foods are responsible to uplift your mood or make you depressed. Deficiency of certain nutrients for a long time can make a person depressed chronically. Certain foods manipulate our moods by affecting neurotransmitters, brain's cell-communicators. Serotonin is one such neurotransmitter which has been used for lifting depression. It is also called happy hormone which makes us feel relaxed.

Dr Simon N. Young of department of psychiatry at McGill University at Montreal says ,' low brain serotonin leads to psychiatric symptoms..' depressed people who attempt suicide , or get into violent activities generally have low levels of serotonin.

My husband needs a good cup of green tea after a tiring session of work in the office. I love tea to reduce stress levels. My friend Renita goes and pops up a chocolate to enhance her mood. Different people like different things to enhance their moods. But one thing is sure that certain eatables definitely play part in uplifting our moods.

**Caffeine:-** Caffeine is known to lift mood that is why coffee with caffeine reduces stress levels. It should be taken in small doses otherwise it can harm our health.

Note:- Caffeine does not suit everybody .

**Spinach:-** Spinach is a rich source of folic acid which is related to moods swings, irritation and lethargy. Dr Young has also said that folic acid deficiency reduces serotonin levels in brain. Deficiency of folic acid for a long time leads to sleeplessness and irritability.

**Grains, cereals, nuts and sea food:-** We get lot of selenium from grains, cereals, nuts and sea food. Brazil nuts are best for selenium; only two nuts can give you your daily dose of it. In recent researched Garlic has been added in the category of mood enhancers (University of Hanover Germany).

> *Tea has up to 10X the polyphenols found in foods like fruits and vegetables*

Foods that trigger Headaches and calms down them:-

Suchitra didn't know that she was allergic to milk. Whenever she ate cheese, paneer or any milk product she used to suffer from migraine. She suffered from one of the worst migraines , where she even used to through up. Once when she went to Lucknow ,one homeopathic doctor told her that she should avoid milk products because she may be allergic to them. For trial bases she stopped having milk products and her migraines also stopped reoccurring.

Another friend of mine was allergic to aginomoto. people are allergic to egg also. So it is difficult to make out what is there which may trigger so mething bad for you.

There can be many reason that we suffer from headaches i.e. lack of sleep, tension, sinus, hunger, too much of noise and stress. In spite of taking pills it does not calm down. Also there are many food items which can trigger the headache. Certain foods are culprit for triggering migraine type of headache. Foods do not act alone they join with two-three more factors to work. They say that headache is genetic but triggered with certain foods.

Many foods contain tyramines and nitrine that trigger neural and blood vessel changes culminating headaches. Chocolates, cheese, red wine, vodka, cottage cheese, baking soda all can be responsible for triggerering headache. It can be any food and the list is long.

**Foods that fights stress:-** Today's lifestyle is the main cause of stress which eventually leads to many kinds of illnesses. Stress has very harmful effects on us. Stressful person can never remain healthy. Either he will not be able to eat well or he will eat more than his appetite. Ailments such as stomach ulcers, blood pressure, digestion, headaches, depression, obesity and immune disorders are all due to continuous stress. When we are stressful, key nutrients of the body start burning fast and we start feeling hunger pangs. There are a few foods which can keep stress away. Foods rich in Vitamin B,Vitamin C, proteins ,Vitamin A and antioxidants. Lentils, chickpeas, quinoa, reduce anxiety and stress.

Vitamin A and C also help during stress. Citrus fruits are full of vitamin C. During stress our body quickly uses the accumulated Vitamin C in our brain tissues and more of Vitamin C is required to keep the level up in the brain. Vitamin C rich fruits and diet help during this time. Vegetables and fruits are also helpful in reducing stress levels. Vegetables, especially green leafy, nuts , milk which are rich source of magnesium are also helpful in reducing stress.

Antioxidants are also known for distressing, hence foods rich in antioxidants help in bringing down stress. During stress free radicals are generated and they are the main cause of cancer. Vegetables which are rich in bio-flavinoids such as broccoli, cauliflower, tomato, cabbage carrots protect cells from free radicals.

Papaya, red bell peppers, basil, arugula, all are very good for removing stress. Sunflower seed which contain folate are also good to eat. Green tea, Chamomile tea, is also an anti- stress agent. It is full of polyphones which are known to protect against stress. it also induces sleep.

Brahmi is a herb which is very potent in distressing.

# CHAPTER 8
# Wonder foods

> Moisten your wheat that the angle of water may enter it
>
> ***Essene -Gospel of Peace***

- Ramya ,a 45 years old bank employ attended a program on healthy eating and has added sprouts in her diet. She is feeling very healthy since then.

- Kiran's mom takes curds regularly twice a day and at the age of 75 she goes for a swim and is very active. She gives the credit of her active life to curd and fermented food.

- Buttermilk is consumed throughout India in some or the other form.

- Majula has been diagnosed with cancer at first stage. Doctors have told her to take wheat germ and soya in the form of flour . In olden times soya was a very popular seed. But over the years with modern lifestyle people forgot about it. Of late there was so much talk about soya as a complete food. People are turning back to soya.

There are many such wonderful food items which have suddenly made their place on the food platter of Indians. This has happened because of awareness, youngsters taking up jobs as chefs, nutritionist, food specialist, dieticians and food decorators etc. It seems as if we Indians had totally forgotten about them. lets know about them and their good qualities.

## 1. Sprouts

Sprouting is also known as germination because extra vitamins are produced during this process of germination. In germination vitamin C level increases up to 10 folds and riboflavin, nicotinic and thiamine level also increases. Iron of germinated foods is easily absorbed by our body. One thing which is very important is that some of the anti-nutrition factors of certain type in pulses are also destroyed. Certain food items after germination are better digested by our body.

We can sprout all types of pulses such as moong, kidney beans, horsegram, peas, chana, all types of grains such as bajra, jowar, raji etc. Soak them in a bowl overnight and next day strain out water and keep them in muslin cloth. Tie them nicely and hang them. Within 12 to 15 hours food item will be germinated nicely. It may take less or more time according to the weather condition depending it is warm or cold. These days market is full of vessels which are used for sprouting food items.

Note: one of the best source to get much more nutrition from a particular food item in natural way.

By the way all Indian household are much familiar with sprouted food.

## 2. Fermentated Food

Fermented food is the food which has live bacteria in it which turns nutrients like sugar and cellulose into amino acids and vitamins. They fight pathogenic bacteria and prevent us from many types of infections. They are also called probiotic foods.

> *Sprouting is a very cheap method of getting vitamins, minerals and enzymes all together in one go. They have all the constituent nutrients of fruits and vegetables in them. This is live food which is free of pesticides.*

Once again it is a natural way to get many folds advantage from foods. Setting milk to curd is one example of fermentation. All over India fermented food is used in different ways. In south regions of India , ground rice and pulses are fermented to make idlis and dosas. In western India khaman Dhokla is also a fermented food. Northern India bhatura is fermented food.

Fermentation generally increases the levels of thiamine, riboflavin and nicotinic acids. Enzymes produced during fermentation are helpful in digestion. Fermented food is spongy and soft and is easily digestible.

## 3. Wheat germ:-

The germ is that part of the wheat grain which helps in reproducing the plant. It is very high in nutrients. Wheat flour which we consume daily is devoid of germ and bran. Many times it is removed from the wheat to make health suppliments. Wheat germ is a powerhouse of nutrients. It is rich source of folate, thiamine, magnesium, manganese, iron, potassium, selenium, phosphorus, zinc, and essential omega-3 fatty acids . It is an excellent source of fibre, minerals, vitamin E, protein,omega-3 fatty acids, Complex Carbohydrates and calcium.

It contains octacosonal which improves mental agility and alertness. There is a compound in our body called homocysteine. It is said that lower levels of homocysteine lower the risk of heart disease, osteoporosis bone fractures, and dementia. Folic acid reduces this compound called homocysteine. Wheat germ also contains a phytonutrient called L-ergothioneine which is a powerful antioxidant that is not destroyed by cooking.

Wheat germ goes rancid easily because it contains unsaturated fats. You can keep it in refrigerator for at least 6 months. It can also be kept for a longer period in roasted form.

## 4. Curd:-

Since time immemorial curds( yoghurt) has been known as immunity increasing food. It is very good for any kind of stomach disorder. It is so good that it can even prevent cancer. The lactobacillus organisms in curds can stimulate the natural killer cells towards attacking the cancer cells. In whatever form it is consumed such as curry, gravy or marinades, it remains beneficial for us.

Curd has no sugars, no carbohydrates and no trans fats but still is the healthiest food with abundance of benefits. It contains friendly bacteria which are very good for our system and hence should be consumed regularly. I have seen people who lived 100-120 years; they made curd integral part of their regular diet.

Though made out of milk by fermenting it, curd is more nutritious than the milk. It is a rich source of vitamins, proteins and calcium. Due to the 20% calcium content, it strengthens our bones. It is good to deal with osteoporosis. It has friendly bacteria so it keeps our digestive system healthy by coping with stomach problems. Consumption of curd is proven beneficial for individuals suffering from dysentery It is very beneficial for strengthening the immune system. As it does not have trans fats, it does not let the cholesterol level to go high. It also reduces the risk of high blood pressure. Women take it to get rid of vaginal infection. All over India people make butter milk and lassi from curd which is supposed to be more beneficial than curd itself and also very good for digestion. It improves the quality of the semen. According to ayurveda regular consumption of curd may cause obesity. Lactic acid of yoghurt is a perfect medium to maximize calcium absorption. Calcium is very essential for the healing of ulcers. Since the absorption of calcium is double with the curd consumption as compared to the milk, is gives much relief from the pain and discomfort due to ulcers. Therefore, curd has anti-ulcer property and it is an excellent remedy for stomach irritation. For mental health Curd cures migraine and the biotin, a vitamin present in the curd is very important for mental health.

**Note:-**

1. Curd should be used fresh as stale curd can cause a lot of side effects such as diarrhea, vomiting, and abdominal cramping. Curd should be consumed within 8 hours after it is set. Avoid taking at night, still if you have to take make sure you add pepper and salt in it.

   You must brush your teeth after consuming curd at night because some of the acid and bacteria in curd can produce a certain amount of damage on teeth.

Do not eat if suffering from fever, cough, asthma or tonsils.

2. Avoid the consumption of curd along with fish and beef as they are contrary foods.

3. If taken in excess it causes constipation.

4. If you are taking any antibiotic, then taking it along with curd is very beneficial as it decreases or thwarts the incidence of antibiotic-related diarrhea.

> *Curds with honey are considered as amrit ( nectar) in Hindu Scriptures. Curd is very good in any form, shreekhund, mishtidoi, dadhi or dahi . one who eats curds daily increases his longivity.*

## 5. Buttermilk:-

Buttermilk is made from curd. It is part of regular diet in Indian houses. Butter milk contains very low fat ,almost zero.

It is a probiotic food. It contains microorganisms which become active once they enter our intestines. This means they are healthy bacteria which are beneficial for our health. They help in improving our digestion and boost our immunity. These bacteria develop vitamins and nutrients in our body. They also protect us from diseases related to heart and cancerous growth. It is rich source of calcium, riboflavin and potassium.

Buttermilk is easily digestible. It is more nutritious than even juices. It tastes better when salt, pepper, green coriander and mint is added to it. It is very rich in calcium. In protein it is as rich as milk. Buttermilk is better than curds.

## 6. Garlic:-

one of the most important and wonder herb of 20th century. Infact since ages people have been using garlic in various forms for various benefits but science has acknowleged its benefits only now. From wearing it around their neck to keeping itbesides the dead bodies in coffin and consuming for various ailments such as pimples, heart problems, wounds,snakebite etc.

Garlic contains allicin which is pungent and gives smell on crushing. It contains active sulphur which has antibacterial qualities. The first and formost benefits from garlic is that it prevents blood clotting and thus reduces the possibility of strokes. Garlic has anti-oxidant properties and reduces cholesterol level which makes it beneficial for heart patients. It prevents LDL from beings oxidized. Garlic works against free radicals. It is very good for the skin. we can use it as anti aging agent. People have been using it in cold and flu since ages without any side effects. It is very effective in acne, pimples, and blemishes. It is a very good cleanser for our system. garlic is known for its anti-carcinodenic properties. It prevents cancerous compounds from forming and developing into tumors. It boosts our metabolism rate and helps sluggish digestion to speed up. It also regulates blood sugar levels in our body. It strengthen our immune system against tumors and ulcers. In olden times people used it to increase the weight of babies still in womb. Even for children, they used to tie garlic pods strung in a thread in their neck. It helps in throwing out the lead and mercury from our system.

## How to consume:-

1. Raw garlic should be consumes early morning with warm water.

2. More than 2/3 cloves should not be taken.

3. if you are already having garlic stop it before any surgery as it thins the blood. Ask your doctor what to do.

4. Asthma patients should not use it this way, it may prove bad for them as it can worsen the condition.

5. cooked garlic has less benefits than the raw one.

6. single bulb garlic is many folds more potent.

> *Rich in vitamins, natural milk sugars and minerals whey water is useful in dysentery and jaundice.*

## 7. Tulsi:-

Tulsi which holds an important place in Hindu religion, is the only plant worshiped as well as used in food by Indians. It is mentioned in the holy scriptures that one kilometer area around the plant basil (Tulsi) gets purified by the presence of this plant. Such is the quality of this plant.

Famous as basil in western parts of the world tulsi is not a new name for Indian householders There are two types of tulsi, white and black. Both have medicinal properties.

> *It is among top 15 medicinal plants in ayurveda. Every part of tulsi is used in herbal medicines. It is truly a wonder herb.*

Tulsi is being used in tea since long. People use the oil to keep away insects and bacteria. The herb has rejuvenating properties. It helps in boosting stamina and endurance. The leaves are used as a nerve tonic. They sharpen our memory and stimulate thought process. Tulsi is antioxidant, anti bacterial, muscle relaxant, antifertility, anti viral, adaptogenic and immunity boosting. Problems related to high blood pressure and high cholesterol can be treated with Tulsi. It is recommended to remove phlegm from the body. Tulsi provides a healthy support during winters when diseases like cough, sneezing and other common cold symptoms prevail. Also it does not have any side effects. Tulsi can effectively cure hormonal imbalance. During fever one can give use decoction of tulsi or can have tulsi tea.

It diminishes the quantity of acids in the blood and strengthens the veins and arteries. Such people are advised to have a daily intake of juice prepared from the extracts of Tulsi. Tulsi is supposed to help in the condition of kidney stones. It has a significant contribution in strengthening the kidneys. People suffering from this problem can prepare a decoction by mixing Tulsi extract with the allovera juice. It makes for an excellent remedy.

Tulsi helps in preventing us from getting infected by ailments. The oil extracted from the Karpoora tulsi is mostly used in the herbal toiletry. Tulsi proves to be very useful for providing relief from respiratory diseases that include bronchitis and asthma. The detoxification properties of Tulsi help in aiding the digestion process and cleaning the intestines, thus detoxifying the body.

**Antimicrobial:-** Tulsi has antibacterial, antifungal and antiviral properties. It inhibits the growth of E coli, B.anthracis, M.tuberculosis etc. It's antitubercular activity is one-tenth the potency of streptomycin and one-fourth that of isoniazid. Tulsi shorten the course of illness ,effectively in patients with viral hepatitis and encephalic.

**Antimalarial:-** The extracts of tulsi have proven effective in malaria. This repellant action lasts for about 2 hours.

**Anti allergic:-** Tulsi has anti allergic properties. It is very effective in immunological disorders including asthma.

**Anti stress/adaptogenic:-** Tulsi taken in hot water or tea reduces stress.

**Anti fertility:-** Tulsi has ursolic acid which is known to for its anti fertility activities. It does not have any side effects so may be used effectively for anti fertility.

**Anti-inflammatory and anti-bacterial:-** Tulsi has anti-inflammatory and anti-bacterial properties. It is rich source of minerals, nutrients and vitamins.

The juice of the leaves is given in catarrh and bronchitis in children. The plant is said to have carminative, diaphoretic and stimulant properties. Tulsi decoction is used for cough and also as mouth washes for relieving tooth ache. It is good for headache, convulsions, cramps, fevers and cholera.

The drinking of Tulsi tea keeps one free from cough and colds and other ailments associated with 'Kapha' dosha in the body. It is a quick energy drink.

> Tulsi leave should not be chewed raw by men because it may give antifertility effect to them. Tulsi leave should not touch the teeth as some chemical reaction starts taking place which is not good for health. So it should be taken in hot water and tea.

It is exceptionally high in beta-carotene and lutein which help us against damage done by free radicals. It is rich in vitamin A which is essential for vision. It also protects us from lung and oral cavity cancers. In every Indian house, one will find a basil (tulsi) bush planted . Vitamin K is found in basil which is essential for mineralization process in the bones. It can be used in salads ,tea and milk.

## Brahmi:-

The botanical name of Brahmi is Bacopa monniera and is known for its brain power enhancing qualities. People used to treat mental illness in olden times and ayurveda has mention of brahmi. It contains a substance called bacosides which is enhances the efficiency of nerve impulse transmission. They do damage repair of worn-out neurons. In India it is given in various forms. There are hair oils with brahmi in them. Markets are flooded with tonics which have brahmi in them.

Herbs from around the world:- Basil, thyme, rosemary, parsley, chives, sage, sorrel ,oregano, mint, coriander, marjoram, tulsi( both black and white) are all herbs which have digestive properties. They stimulate the production of enzymes that help breakdown food and its absorption. These herbs also contain trace elements which are essential for a healthy body. They are used in salads and chutenis( sauces) . They give fragrances and flavours to food.

## 8. Soya :-

20 years back when I first heard about soya that it is a protein rich food, and soya protein is equal to meat and milk , I started mixing it in the wheat flour.

Soya has the highest amount of protein than any other food. Soya protein is a complete protein. Our body requires 20 amino acids, out of which 11 are produced by our body. The remaining nine we get from different food items. Soya protein is the only one food item which provides all the nine amino acids. Soya protein isolates are a highly digestible source of amino acids.

Soya is full of many types of photochemical. Soya contains nutritionally significant amount of one very essential phytochemicals called isoflavones. They lower cholesterol, reduce menopause symptoms and are anti cancer.

Soya is also very rich source of calcium, mineral, vitamins and dietary fiber. 100 gm of soya contains 88 milligrams of calcium that looks after our daily requirements of calcium. Soya calcium is also easily absorbed by our body. They also contain copper and magnesium minerals along with vitamin B such as niacin, pyridoxine and folacin. As soya is rich in fiber , it reduces risk of cancers and heart problems. Soya is a complete diet which has many fold benefits.

# Wonder Herbs

Poornima had invited a few friends over for a party. She prepared continental fusion food such as pasta, Thai green curry with tofu, Mexican tomato and tortillas, French buerre, cutlets and so many other tasty dishes. No, she didn't have to go abroad to buy the stuff, everything thing is available in India now. Oregano, mint, coriander, marjoram, dill, parsley, chives, sage, sorrel, thyme, rosemary, you name it and it is there in the market. Fresh, with the same fragrance and beneficial qualities. Yes, the way our Indian herbs are full of nutrients these herbs also give us nutrition and medicinal benefit.

Thyme, rosemary, parsley, chives, sage, sorrel, oregano, mint, coriander, marjoram, dill are other herbs which are very important and essential for us as they provide us with minerals, vitamins and other nutrients.

*Dried herbs have stronger flavour than green ones. One teaspoon of dries herbs equals four teaspoons of fresh herbs, as a general rule. Add them in the cooking in the last leg.*

**Rosemary:-** One of the most famous memory-enhancing herbs is rosemary. Just the scent of rosemary stimulates brain activity and improves the performance. Carbonic acid in it dilates the cerebral vascular tissues.

Have tea with rosemary in it. Green tea is antioxidant and contains catechins (found incamellia sinensis) which restore damaged brain cells. Bacopin repairs neurons and improves alertness, memory and cognition. Hawthorn removes toxins from the brain and strengthens tissues. Schisandra improves memory as well as mood. The antioxidants in herbs are vital for health of body cells.

**Thyme:-** It also protects the food from microbial contamination. It is very effective against various types of fungi which infect hair, toe nails and feet. It is used in cough and bronchitis related problems. It is beneficial in skin related problems also. Thyme is also known as anti-oxidant.

Turmeric has great anti-septic properties. Should be taken with milk every night. very good for children who play and get hurt every now and then.

**Parsley:-** It is a rich source of anti-oxidants such as luteolin that combine with reactive oxygen-containing molecules and help prevent oxygen based damage to cells. It also contains nutrients such as vitamin C and A which play important role in preventing many diseases such as cold and cough. Vitamin c is also anti-inflammatory agent. Parsley is rich source of this vitamin. It also contains beta-carotene which is converted to vitamin A by the body. This is also known as' anti-infective vitamin' because it is very good for our immune system. it is also good source of folic acid , which is essential for a healthy heart .

**Chives:-** chives contain minerals, vitamins, flavonoids anti-oxidants and fiber. They are anti-viral, anti-bacterial and anti-fungal. It helps in decreasing stiffness of blood vessels and does not let the blood clot formation. Chives also contain vitamin A and K. infact it contains the highest amount of vitamin K which is helpful in maintaining bone health. Vitamin K also helps in limiting neuronal damage in the brain which shows that it has role in the treatment of Alzheimer's disease. Chives also contain folates and vitamin B along with other minerals.

**Sage:-** sage contains rich amount of anti-oxidants which protect us from the damage of free radicals. It also protects against many age related health problems such as arthritis, macular degeneration and many more. We must have a large variety of anti-oxidants because where one type of anti-oxidant may work in the body the other one can't go and neutralize free radicals that the other one might have missed. It is also anti-inflammatory. People with inflammatory condition should take sage every day. It is also a memory enhancer, sleep inducer and good during menopause.

**Sorrel:-** Sorrel is a good appetizer. It can be used effectively during stomach disorders. An infusion of sorrel leaves is good in bringing down the fever. It is rich in vitamin C and is used effectively in the prevention and treatment of scurvy- which is caused by lack of vitamin C. The juice of the leaves are also used to remove warts. It is a very useful plant based vegetable.

**Oregano:-** A herb from min family, oregano is a rich natural source of vitamin K. It is anti-bacterial, anti-oxidant (42 more than apples) and anti-fungal. It contains important minerals for health, necessary fiber and omega-3 fatty acids.

**Mint:-** Mint has been integral part of Indian kitchen. We have been using it in salads, chutneys, juices, curries and as marinades. It is very good for digestion and hence is good for stomach too. It is a strong diuretic and helps in removing toxins from the body. Mint has many other benefits such as cures asthma, cough and cold. It clears blocked respiratory passage. It is anti-fungal and anti-bacterial. Mint is so cooling for the body that during hot summers it is taken in the form of juice and chutney. It is a good blood cleanser. It also relieves aches and pains. Mint is used in many medicines and drugs very effectively.

**Coriander:-** Coriander is effectively used for the treatment of ulcers, anemia, digestion, swelling, blood sugar disorders, skin disorders and cholesterol. It contains linoleic acid which has anti rheumatic and anti arthritic properties. It also has vitamin. Coriander chutney is useful in stomach disorders. It has cooling effect on the body. Because it is rich source of iron and hence is useful in anemic conditions. It has vitamin A and certain minerals too.

**Marjoram:-** Marjoram contains many phyto-nutrients which are essential for our optimal health. It has anti-inflammatory, anti-oxidant, anti-viral and anti-bacterial properties. It is very high in vitamin C, vitamin A, beta –carotene , which contain very powerful anti-oxidants .Together they all helps in removing free radicals from our body. It is good for healthy immune system. vitamin A also protects us against lung and oral cavity cancers. It also contains vitamin K.

**Dill:-** Dill does not contain cholesterol. It is full of anti-oxidants, vitamins, fibers, folic acid, nacin, beta carotene and minerals. Dill is used in northern parts of India and is known as soye. It contains many essential oils which have medicinal properties. It is so rich in vitamin A that 100 gm of dill provides you 257% of your daily requirement of vitamin A. It is good for skin, lungs, oral cavity, vision and healthy mucus membranes. It is also good for our immune system.

> *Sage protects against many age related health problems such as arthritis, macular degeneration and many more.*

**Ginko (herb)** is so strong that it has been suggested for brain stroke, memory problems, dementia and Alzheimer's. A regular dose shows results within two and a half months.

**How to consume Herbs:-** In a cup ,take a spoon full of herbs and pour boiling water in it. Keep it covered for sometime (3-4 minutes), drain it and drink it. If you want to use them in tincture form, take 20-30 drops half an hour before or after food.

**Note:-** Herbs taken together are more potent, but should be balanced at the same time. They do not tax the adrenals and can be taken safely for a longer time. They do not have side effects.

## Benefits of Seeds

I remember Timsi has just come back from a nature cure residential clinic. Like many other women , every year she also goes to this particular weight loss clinic and stays there for 10 days. Though she losses weight, but within three months she puts on weight again. But this time , what I liked about her was, that she was always carrying some seeds in her purse, which she ate whenever she felt hungry. There were , almonds ,flax seeds , sunflower seeds and walnuts etc. Actually I liked this idea so much that now I too started keeping a few in my purse.

Seeds are rich in protein, antioxidants and have many types of nutrients which are required for good health.

**Flax seed:-** Indian name is Alsi ke beej. A very rich source of omega 3 fatty acids. Omega 3 contains phytoestrogen which is an astrogen substitute, required to stabilize levels of hormone imbalance. It helps in stabilizing blood sugar and you feel less hungry. They also improve immunity and reduce cholesterol levels. Taken as part of meal they work as roughage and prevent constipation.

**Walnut seeds:-** Walnuts are rich in omega 3 fatty acids which make you feel less hungry. They are good for people with diabetes. they reduce inflammation and pain. Very good for brain and adrenal glands.

**Chia seeds:-** Indian name is sabja. They having cooling properties and are used throughout the summers in India. It is used in falooda kulfi, khus sharbat, rose sharbat and badam milk. Soak them for some time and they will turn into jelly like substance and swell into almost double their size. They are a combination of soluble and insoluble fibre thus help stabilize levels of blood sugar.

**Pumpkin seeds:-** Also known as kaddu ke beej, they are flat in size and come with a covering ( peel). From inside they are green in colour. They are rich source of zinc and magnesium. Very useful to keep depression away because they contain T-tryptophan. Recommended for protection against osteoporosis and parasites. Used in kheer, halwa ,thandai and sharbats. Also eaten raw or roasted.

**Sunflowers seeds:-** very rich source of phytochemicals so can be used for losing weight. Some people also eat them with the covering to get fibre from it. As sunflower is rich in copper, selenium folate and vitamin E, hence it is also heart healthy. Use them light roasted as a snack or have them raw, they are surely beneficial for good health.

**Watermelon seeds:-** known as tarbooz ke beej, they are black from outside with a thick cover and after peeling you will find which tasty seeds inside. Rich source of Vitamin B, magnesium, arginine and amino acids they regulate blood pressure and have cooling properties. They are used in puddings, kheer, drinks and can be had raw.

**Nigella seeds:-** Indian name is kalaunji. Most popular use in pickles and sprinkled on Nans. They are very useful in the treatment of breathing problems and asthma. Many people use them as tadak over pulses or sprinkle them on salads.

**Muskmelon seeds:-** known as kharbooje ke beej. They have cooling properties and are used extensively in puddings and salads.

**Sesame seeds:-** They contains rich amount of calcium, magnesium, proteins, vitamins, unsaturated fats and minerals. Used in deserts, puddings and many drinks.

**Almonds:-** almonds are very good for brain and they nourish the vital energy of our body. They are full of calcium, and other minerals. They are alkaline. It is said that almonds should be soaked overnight and taken empty stomach next morning. Daily 7-9 almonds are recommended for alertness and health of brain.

**Pistachio Nuts:-** they purify blood and contain less calories. They also lubricate the intestines and are good for removing constipation.

**Brazil nuts:-** They are rich source of amino acids and selenium. They are good for our immunity.

**Hazelnuts:-** They strengthen stomach and are full of minerals such as iron, potassium, folic acid and vitamin E.

**Note:-** All the nuts, grains and seeds should be soaked before consuming. Soaking neutralizes enzyme inhibitors , which are present in all the seeds. This encourages the production of numerous beneficial enzymes. This is a method of increasing their vitamins. During the process of soaking and fermenting, gluten and other difficult-to-digest proteins are partially broken down into simpler components that are more readily available for absorption. This process also removes or reduce phytic acid in grains. It also prevents mineral deficiencies and bone loss.

# Spices

Since I was a child , I have been seeing people around me using spices for minor problems. I too have used ajwain and asafoetida many times .

Since time immemorial people have been using spices in their cooking. They have many qualities and give quick benefit to us. Spices such as coriander, caraway, aniseed, cardamom, fennel, cumin, dill, star anise, and asafoetida help in digestion. Some of them are useful in releasing trapped gases in our stomach. They give good aroma, fragrances and flavours to food. A small amount (half a tea spoon) is enough to give good taste.

**Aniseed:-** A great digestive. Used for indigestion, nausea, bloating of stomach. It is anti-oxidant and anti-inflammatory.

**Ajwain:-** medicinal value. Digestive qualities. Good for liver functioning and wind in stomach.

**Asafetida:-** good for digestion.

**Coriander:-** good for nerves.

> *Jeera added in water( Jeera Water) is very good in flatulance, dyspepsia, and cold.*

**Caraway:-** prevents bloating in stomach.

**Cardamom:-** good for throat, teeth and heart. freshens bad breath. Cures blood pressure.

**Cumin:-** good for digestion. gives strength. Enhances lost appetite. Should be used in all food.

**Cloves:-** antibiotic , good for digestion, pain reducing.

**Cinnamon:-** Improves digestion .also gives aroma to food.

**Cress:-** good for skin and thyroid gland.

**Dill:-** prevents wind formation. Useful in colic pain among babies. Used for post delivery problems.

**Fennel:-** used in herbal tea and desserts. Cures diarrhoea.

**Fenugreek:-** very good for diabetics people. Strengthen nerves. Good for hair. Has medicinal value.

**Ginger Dry:-** improves appetite. Good for liver.

**Kalonji:-** gives relief during menstrual pain.

**Mustard:-** used in many medicines. Is antibiotic and pain relieving? Good for skin and hair.

**Nutmeg:-** give flavour to food. Good for brain and nerves. Cures menstrual problems and sexual disorders.

**Pepper:-** good for cough and cold.

**Salt:-** besides sea salt there are two types of salts. Rock salt also known as sendha namak and black salt known as kala namak. Both are rich source of minerals. Black salt contains iron and sulphur in it. Good for digestion.

**Saffron:-** Antiseptic, antidepressant, anti-oxidant, digestive, anti-conversant. It is also rich in minerals. It also provides many volatile oils , the most important one is safaranl, which gives it its colour.

**Turmeric:-** many medicinal qualities. Anti-allergic, anti-inflammatory, antibiotic. One of the best spices.

## Continental secrets

**Shiitake mushrooms:-** common name is Japanese mushroom, black forest mushroom ,golden oak mushroom. They are used in many herbal remedies. Research has shown that they are antitumor and help in lowering cholesterol level in our body. They also boost immune system and help in stopping viruses from multiplying. These mushrooms contain a compound called lentinan which is believed to stop the growth of tumours. They also contain another compound eritadenine which lowers cholesterol by not letting it absorb into blood. But this claim is still under study.

Shiitake mushrooms were being used in china as medicine during 100AD and they are still being used in their food. The effects and potency of these mushrooms lies in the way they are prepared.

**Glutathione:-** it is naturally produced in all the body cells to fight free radicals. As one grows older, their production also start reducing and immunity starts decreasing. If food rich in glutathione is consumed regularly , body immunity can be regenerated. Natural source of glutathione is fresh vegetables and fruit. Fruits are generally taken raw but vegetables are cooked before consuming. Some amount of glutathione is lost while cooking but left over is still useful for us. Broccoli, spinach, tomato, cabbage, walnuts are all rich source of glutathione.

**Gingko Bilobo:-** gingko is very for brain and heart. It improves blood circulation. It has unique property of making blood squeeze through the tiniest of blood vessels. It helps improve memory and brain power. It prevents blood clotting. Also by dilating blood vessels it stimulates blood circulation. Anybody after the age of 50 can take gingko but after consulting doctor. Doctors even recommend it to prevent memory loss at a later age and relief from muscle pain. It is a very good antioxidant.

**Evening primrose:-** this herb has become very popular recently. The oil extracted from primrose seeds is a potent source of essential fatty acids. It is well known for female related problems such as premenstrual problems and menopause related issues. It is good for skin also. It has a substance called gamma-linoleic acid which is helpful in arthritis and some eczemas.

**Echinacea:-** it is also known as purple coneflower. This herb is very good for immune system. if taken regularly for a month it certainly and surely boosts immune system. it is also known to boost resistance against infection and ailments.

**Alfalfa:-** another wonder herb is alfalfa. It is full of nutrients. People generally take it in sprouted form which is very high in vitamins and minerals. We use it in salads also.

**Kelp:-** very rich in iodine which is good our health. People who are having thyroid gland related should have kelp as it is a tonic for thyroid gland . Also it aids sluggish metabolism.

**Ginseng:-** Ginseng improves memory, mental and physical health. It can be effectively used to help in erectile dysfunction, hepatitis, menopause and blood pressure. It also reduces stress levels and fatigue. They say it is anti-aging and keep one young and cheerful. There are many types of ginseng. It is also a remedy for cough and cold. It is one of the most used herbs in the world.

---

*The best and cheapest way to get Vitamin D is sun light. 20 minutes exposure to the sun early morning is enough for your daily need of this vitamin.*

---

**Olives:-** Olives constitute one of the world's largest fruit crops, with more than 25 million acres of olive trees planted worldwide. We all have heard about the qualities and benefits of olive oil. But very less is known about having olives raw, pickled, salad and as a vegetable. Olive tree lives for hundreds of years.

Olive has been used as a medicinal plant in Greece since long. They know the benefits of this fruit. Olive leaves have been used in treatment of inflammatory problems. Olives provide us with anti-inflammatory benefits, especially during circumstances involving allergy. Olives have high content of monounsaturated fats which help in decreasing blood pressure. The oleic acid found in olives after getting absorbed into the body and transported to our cells, can change signaling patterns at cell membrane level . These changes at cell membrane level result in decreased blood pressure.

Olives contains some of the key phytonutrients that make them unique as an antioxidant-rich food. Oleuropein, found exclusively in olives also works as an antioxidant nutrient in many ways. It decreases oxidation of LDL cholesterol and lowers many types of oxidative stress and also helps in protecting nerve cells from oxidation. Olives contains another phytonutrient named Hydroxytyrosol which has been linked to prevent growth of cancer. It is also supposed to be preventing bone loss. It seems to be true because Mediterranean Diet which includes olives as its integral part has long been associated with decreased risk of osteoporosis.

Olives are a remarkable source of antioxidant and anti-inflammatory phytonutrients. The phytonutrient content of olives depends upon many factors such as the variety of olives, stage of maturation, and treatment given after the harvest. Olives are a very good source of monounsaturated fat and a good source of iron, copper, and dietary fiber.

# CHAPTER 9
# Food Rainbow

'Artificial colours contribute towards many behavioral problems in human beings. They cause many health problems.'

Ritika fainted in the class and her teacher informed her mother Aarti about it. Aarti picked up car keys and in no time reached her school. As she reached school, she found that Ritika was ok and resting in the MI Room. After picking up her Ritika, she rushed to the doctor. Ritika was anaemic. Doctor told Aarti not to worry but should change her daughter's diet. She was advised to have pomegranate, tomato , spinach and all types of fruits and vegetables. Pomegranate is specially good in building blood. Ritika started eating fruits and vegetables of all colours . within six months she was normal. In fact we should add fruits and vegetables of all different colours.

## Role of colour therapy in food

Based on research of World Cancer Fund and Better Health Foundation food has been divided into different groups of 5 different colours to get maximum benefits from natural food. According to this theory we must consume all 5 colours of food in a day. All the seven colours of the spectrum are also in our body. When a certain colour becomes deficient in our body, we fall sick. Fruits and vegetables are of different colours and each colour is related to a different pytochemical which is essential for us. We should extract full benefit of from all the colours. They are as important for us as vitamins and minerals. Here we are not talking about artificial colours for example banana has natural yellow colour which is good for us.

## Main food colours:-

### 1. Red:-

Red colour vegetables and fruits get their colour because of natural plant pigments called lycopene or anthocyanins . They prevent formation of blood clotting and protect against heart disease. They contain lycopene which is an antioxidant and also improves blood circulation. They also contain ellagic acid , hesperidin andquercetin which are known to reduce the risk of prostate cancer and other growth related to tumors. They also support join tissue in cases of arthritis.

onions (red ones), radish, tomato, strawberry, cherry, red pepper, salmon fish, kidney beans, sweet potato, beetroot, raspberries , red grapes, pomegranates, red cabbage, cranberries , rhubarb and watermelon.

### 2. Orange/yellow:-

Yellow /orange fruits and vegetables get their colour because they contain natural plant pigment called carotenoids which makes these vegetables and fruits rich source of beta-carotene. It is required by our body to make vitamin A which helps in maintaining healthy mucous membranes and healthy eyes.

They also provide us vitamin C, lycopene, potassium and flavonoids. These nutrients reduce age related problems such as macula degeneration and risk of prostate cancer. They fight against free radicals and good for health of bones.

We can obtain yellow/orange colour from oranges, apricots, melons, corn, peaches, mangoes, yellow pepper, bananas, pumpkin, sweet potatoes, carrots, lemons, sweet corns papayas, and mangoes.

Oranges and other citrus do not have much vitamin A but have abundance of vitamin C and folate which reduce the risk of birth defects.

## 3. White:-

Fruits and vegetables of white colour are rich source of beta-glucans, EGCS,SDG, lidnans that make our immune system strong by supporting white blood cells. They are also rich in antioxidants and reduce cholesterol levels. They regulate blood pressure in our body and also help in preventing cancer. chicken, fish, paneer, tofu (beancurd), cauliflower, potato, onions, white beans etc.

## 4. Green:-

Green vegetables get their colour because of chlorophyll. This colour is very good for our eyes and skin. Green vegetables contain calcium and vitamin c which boosts our immune system. Dark green leafy vegetables contain lutein which works with another chemical, zeaxanthin to keep our eyes healthy. Together they may reduce the risk of age –related macular degeneration which if not treated, can lead to blindness. The whole cabbage family is rich source of indoles which may help protecting against certain cancers. It is a rich source of folate which reduces the risk of birth related defects. We get this colour from spring onions, spinach, green pepper ,beans, green grapes, cucumber, green cabbage,kiwi fruit, salad leaves, ladyfinger , broccoli , peas ,artichocks, asparagus and green fenugreek etc.

5. **Blue/violet:-**

Blue fruits and vegetables get their colour from plant pigment anthocyanins. This pigments is obtained by eating blue colour fruits and vegetables such as blueberry, blackberry, raisins, black grapes, dates, red cabbage( Chinese cabbage), brinjol, passion fruit, mangostean. This is a powerful anti-oxidant which protects cells damage. They also reduce risk of cancer, stroke and heart disease. They help in improving the memory function. Figs, plums, blueberries, raisins, purple grapes, eggplant and prunes are rich source of this colour.

*'We use Monosodium Glutamate to enhance the flavour of food and use it in Chinese cooking. It is known to cause obesity, diabetes, triggers epilepsy, destroys eye tissues . one should avoid it.'*

## Seasons and food:-

*'Never eat any leafy vegetable during rainy season as it can get contaminated easily.'*

*Heeran was very fond of leafy green vegetables. She used to have spinach, cabbage and other leafy vegetables regularly. She had made it a point to wash vegetables thoroughly before cooking. Even during rainy season she used to consume spinach. Once she was admitted in the hospital for stomacache. The doctor told her that she needed deworming. It happened after rainy season. There are a lot of microscopic germs hidden in the leaves of leafy vegetables.*

Food which is available during a particular season is perfect natural food for that season. Nature has made different foods for different seasons. What is easily produced during summers will not be easily produced during winters.

During Shishir the weather is cold and during this weather one should have bitter food. Vasant (basant) or spring is the season when winters are coming to their end. Weather is pleasant and astringent is the right food for spring. After vasant it starts warming up and summer arrives. Sun also slowly starts increasing its heat. Khatta food has been prescribes for summers. Summer is followed by varsha. Sour food is recommended for varsha or rainy season. Next is sharat season or autumn , when one should have salty food. Last is hemant season when one should consume sweet food.

During Hemant and Shishira season sweet, salty and sour food can be consumed. During this time digestive activity becomes more powerful. Wind formation in the stomach also increases. To reduce wind in the body sweet, salty and sour food should be consumed. Wheat , gramflour, jowar, bajra, maize , sugarcane, jaggary should be part of diet.

Vasant season liquifies increased kapha because of warm sun. It becomes cause of diseases. This is the time one should have fermented food, barley, honey with water. One should not quickly change over to cold food.

Grishma season is the time when vata starts increasing and kapha starts decreasing. Sun becomes harsh and make one feel giddy. Curd, buttermilk and plenty of fresh water should be consumed. Rice is also recommended. Lot of fruits should be eaten.

Varsha ( rainy) season is the time when digestive activity weakens. We should take food that enhances digestive activity. Soups and easily digestible food should be consumed.

Sharat season is dominated by pitta. One should have bitter, astringent and sweet food. Avoid oily, fried and heavy food which is not easy to digest.

We must balance pitta with drinking lot of water, juice, buttermilk, lassi, watermelon etc. pitta resides in stomach and liver so these organs should be cooled with cool liquids. You can add rose water to your drinks. Avoid spicy and hot food such as meat and non vegetarian food. Lot of green vegetables and pulses should be consumed. Also avoid acidic food.

Pitta has dominance during 10 am to 2 pm . so your lunch should be your major meal as this time of the day pitta is the strongest and food digest fast. Kapha time should be your sleep time as during this time you will be able to sleep easily.

If we live according to nature, nature will give support with its own healing powers.

# Vegetarian v/s Non Vegetarian Food

Swati is very fond of non-vegetarian food. But it does not suit her stomach. She suffers from constipation after having non-vegetarian food. Her sister Sujata likes only vegetarian food. It is by choice , no body forces her to eat vegetarian food. She feels vegetarian food suits her constitution. Also she does not like to kill animals for her food when God has given so many other things to eat. She likes to have natural, fresh food .

This debate is on since time immemorial, whether one should be vegetarian or non vegetarian. Today more and more people are converting to vegetarians all over the world. Some of them who have gone to the extent of not having milk because it is animal product are called Vegan.

Man is a vegetarian by nature because body organs are developed to digest vegetarian food. First of all we see that nature has equipped us with teeth which are designed to crush, chew and grind. Where as animals have teeth to tear raw flesh. Saliva of humans is alkaline and helpful in digestion of plant protein where as animal food is acidic forming and is not easy to digest. It causes unhealthy putrefaction bacteria in our intestines. Our liver cannot through excess uric acid which is produced by the breakdown of animal protein where as animals stomach produces hydrochloric acid which makes digestion of animal proteins easier. our intestines are very long ( 27''), they can digest only veg food. Non veg food takes log to digest and keeps lying in the intestine and stars rusting. Where as animals' intestines are only 8'', and make the process of digestion short. Also meat does not get clogged, it travels the intestine soon and is out of the system.

Never have water after having watermelon , muskmelon. It may lead to diarrhoea. It also dilutes digestive juices which makes the absorption of food difficult.

But still the non veg. market flourishes day by day. People who are non vegetarian believe that all the proteins and nutrients are available in animal food. Let's see the truth.

All vegetables, fruits, grains, seeds, cereals come under the name of vegetarian diet. Vegetarian diet is rich in fiber, many types of vitamins, minerals, trace elements, folate, proteins, natural sugars, enzymes. Green leafy vegetables contain antioxidants also.

**Benefits of non vegetarian food:-** There are certain benefits of non-veg food like certain vitamin such as B12, which aids in the production of red blood cells, the digestion and assimilation of nutrients in foods and the protection of nerve endings, is available in animal products ( meats, eggs, seafood) in abundance. Though it is available in soya products, dairy products and fortified cereals also but meat is a rich source of vitamin B12. Meat, chicken , fish and eggs have iron, zinc , calcium in abundance. Meat has lot of protein and all the essential amino acids which our body requires. People who are into sports require protein rich diet otherwise they can become anaemic. Also we should add some amount of fat in our diet as it is required for normal functioning of our body.

**Omega-3 Fatty Acids:-** non-vegetarian food offers much higher level of omega-3 fatty acids than vegetarian food. Omega-3 Fatty Acids are helpful in lowering bad cholesterol levels ,reduce the risk of heart disease. They also keep the arteries unblocked. They help in brain development and function. Though we get omega-3 fatty acids from flaxseeds and other vegetables but the amount is not sufficient.

Phosphorus which we get from cereals and legumes doesn't get absorbed as easily as the one we get from meat. Sportsman and bodybuilders are required to have protein rich diet and they are recommended to have non-veg diet.

But still I would say that benefits of being vegetarians are much more.

## Benefits of a vegetarian food

Vegetarian food is very effective in preventing the progression of coronary artery disease. Because vegetables are low in fats, they minimize the risk of cholesterol and fats in body .It are helpful in maintaining good health and at the same time keep our weight under check. We remain away from the risk of weight related problems such as heart disease, stroke and diabetes. As a result lowers the risk of heart problems, blood pressure, gall bladder stones and kidney stones, diabetes and many types of cancer. As vegetables are rich source of high fibre, our digestive system also remains healthy.

There are many vegetables which have cancer-protective qualities. Cabbage, carrots, broccoli, celery, dill, parsley, tomatoes, grapes, blue berries, beans, oats, flaxseeds, whole wheat, nuts, garlic, chives, ginger, turmeric, thyme, basil ,Indian tulsi, oregano, rosemary etc. are all anti cancerous. All these herbs contains, carotenoids, flavonoids, phytosterols, sulfide compounds , isoflavones and many other such elements.

WHO and some other groups point out that vegetarian diets provide us complete nutrition which we need today. According to a research eight food groups have been identified which have cancer preventive qualities. And all are from plant kingdom.

There is a place in Japan, Okinawa , which has longest life expectancy in the world according to a 30-year study on these people. They eat low-calorie diet of unrefined complex carbohydrates, soy and fiber-rich fruits and vegetables.

 CHAPTER 10

# Wisdom of The Ages

Food surely protects from the health problems. But if your eating habits, knowledge about food, life style is not correct , even the

healthiest food will also fail to protect you.

Let's do one exercise:-

Try to remember the food your grandmother used to cook. Remember the taste. Do you know why it tasted so sumptuous ? Your grand mother went and bought those fruits and vegetables herself. She washed them , removed the dirt and cooked on slow fire . All this she did herself. There was no dust particles in that food. And you never got tired eating that home cooked food again and again.'

We must follow a few rules to get healthy food.

> 'We must wash the vegetables properly before cooking so that all the pesticides and dirt can be removed completely. Pesticides are designed to withstand even rain, hence washing only with water will not be enough. Soak for 10 minutes. use salt and vinegar to wash vegetables.'

# Know your food

- Buy vegetables which are fresh, bright in colour and feel heavy in your hands.

- Vegetables and fruits which have spots, blemishes, rotten, fungal mold should not be bought.

- Buy only seasonal vegetables and fruits , they have maximum nutrients.

- Include all colours of vegetables and fruits in your diet yellow, orange, green, light green, white etc.

- Buy in small quantities so that you can consume them within one or two days.

- We should wash vegetables thoroughly with salt water for some time so that any kind of dust, residue of chemical sprays , pesticides or any sand particles are removed. Green vegetables have short shelf life and start rottening soon so use them as soon as possible.no point eating unfit vegetables.

- Buy in small quantity so that you can use them within two three days.

- If you keep them for a longer period their health benefits and nutrients start reducing.

- If you are storing them in refrigerator, keep them in plastic wraps which have holes in them. Do not cut and keep.

# How to buy food items

It is not necessary that more expensive foods are more nutritious also. Many times cheaper foods are rich source of nutrients.

1. Buy seasonal fruits as they are much cheaper. Mangoes and orange when in season should be preferred than costly fruits such as apple or pears. Orange, guava, papaya are cheaper. Apple should be eaten when they are in season. They will be cheaper that time. Guava is poor man's fruit but it is very rich in vitamin C. even amla is also cheap and best in vitamin C.

2. Do not through away leaves some of the vegetables such as raddish, beetroot and carrots. They are full of minerals and vitamins.

3.  Wheat, rice and corn are good foods , at the same time jowar, bajra, ragi, unpolished rice are cheaper and nutritious. So add them also in your diet.

4. Have mixed pulses as they will go you all kinds of nutrients.

5. Jaggery is cheaper and better than sugar which is not good for health.

6. Instead of having bulky food such as rice and dal which fill and swell the stomach, have combination of two or three things. You can add palak in pulses or have sprouted pulses.

7. Vegetables which contain vitamin C should be eaten raw because Vitamin C is lost during cooking or boiling.

8. Must include green mint and coriander chutney in your diet daily. It is has good nutritional value.

9. Do not use soda while cooking to preserve colour of the vegetables as it destroys vitamins.

## Cooking Habits:-

"No one who cooks, cooks alone. Even at her most solitary, a cook in the kitchen is surrounded by generations of cooks past, the advice and menus of cooks present, the wisdom of cookbook writers."

*— Laurie Colwin*

1. Boil rice in just enough water . when we boil rice in more water and through away excess water, even the nutrients are also thrown away with the water. So let the water get absorbed in rice.

2. Cook pulses and vegetables in small amount of water , better if you steam them. If some water if left after boiling keep it sepate and after cooling it, use it to knead flour so that the vitamins and minerals are also used.

3. Carrots, amla,radish, cucumber and vegetables which contain vitamin C should not be boiled, eat them raw. Vitamin C is lost during cooking and boiling.

4. Green leafy vegetables such as palak, methi etc should be nice washed to remove any dirt particles and then cooked in no extra water because they contain enough water in them to get cooked. Cover vessel with lid while cooking.

5. First boil water and then put vegetables in them , not the other way that putting them in cold water and then boiling.

6. Do not use soda baking Soda during cooking to keep the colour of vegetables intact, it will destroy all the nutrients.

7. Use of pressure cooker is good as it encourages covered and quick cooking and preserves nutrients.

8. Use of lemon juice, tamarind, curd or buttermilk is also good as it reduced the loss of vitamins and minerals while cooking ( not true for Vitamin C based vegetables).

## Combining of foods for better nutrition:

One can always combine different classes of foods to get maximum nutrition.

1. Cereals like wheat or rice can be combined with pulses to get more and variety of proteins.

2. Two or more cereals can also be combined for maximum nutrients. Wheat and corn atta or wheat, corn, ragi, grams flour,soya which is called pachrangi are examples.

3. Combine food items from all the five groups to get maximum nutrients. Also include raw food such as salads.

4. Must make parboiled rice part of your diet. You may take it twice a week, it will certainly make difference.

5. Parched food such as porridge is very good form

of diet. The starch in it is easy to digest and nutritive value also increases.

6. Puffed food such as mumure ( muri, layie) , popcorn should also be made part of diet. Do not add any butter in it.

> *Water kept in copper vessel over night, and taken early morning empty stomach. it is believed to prevent asthma and cure respiratory problems.*

**One** of my uncles, who was a doctor had a very peculiar way of treating his patients. As soon as a patient arrived, he used to give him a dose of castor oil and make him sit for half an hour. Then direct his patient to loo. After that he used to start his treatment.

He always said that all ailments start from digestion , it could be over digestion, under digestion, constipation etc. For this we should develop good food habits.

## Eating habits:-

1. Food should be cooked with love and care.

2. It should also be served and eaten with love and in congenial atmosphere.

3. Wash your hands properly and thank God before eating.

4. Chew your food properly so that your digestive system does not have to work hard.

5. Drink water or any other liquid half an hour before or after your meals. Do not take milk or any kind of juice with food.

6. When eating fill 2/3 of your stomach so that digestion of the food is easy in your stomach. Undigested food becomes toxic and leads to ailments.

7. There should be a gap of 4-5 hours between meals. Not even short eats because our system has to work in digesting that too.

8. Bath should be taken before meals. If one has to it should be 3 hours after meals.

9. Yoga or any kind of exercise should be done three hours after the meals.

10. Do not eat when depressed or angry ,both times digestion becomes less effective .

## Body is Temple

*One must fast once in 15 days. It cleanses and gives rest to the system.*

## Detoxifying:-

Toxins enter in our body by food, water and environment. Our money minting food industry is providing us with poisonous artificial chemicals everyday. Artificial colours , which are described as aluminium lake colours, are used to make food more attractive. They are created on a substrate of hydrated aluminium. For your knowledge this is added into products with a low water content such as cakes, pastries and biscuits.

Many types of bread which is available on shelf contains flour enhancers/improvers ( they do not specify on the label), which can be potassium bromated, which is proven carcinogen. Many of the readymade foods also contain emulsifier, lethicin and hydrolyzed protein and it could be thermally oxidized soya beans which is culprit of hormonal changes which causes thyroid dysfunction.

These alter our metabolism and disrupt our finely balanced neurotransmitters as well as harmons, which results in making us depressed and we take to sickness. Not all the chemicals are bad for our health. Chemicals added in tap water and common table salt are good for us. But rest of the chemicals are really damaging our health. They are added to enhance appearance, taste and shelf life of harmful foods. Only the manufacturer is being benefitted by these.

If we think home food is the best, hold on, we cannot rely on the so called fresh, green leafy vegetables any more. They are not giving us our quota of potassium, magnesium, sodium, zinc, calcium and other essential minerals. So many pesticides are sprinkled on the crop that we may be consuming more of pesticides than vegetables. To get more produce from the crop farmers are using many other products.

All these things toxify our body. These toxins weaken our immune system. We are not eating nourishing food. Our food is feeding us with more of poison. Eventually our energy levels drop down, we fall sick. Here are a few tips to keep your body toxin free and ealthy.

# Detoxify:-

Detoxification of the vegetables and ourselves is a must.

1.  First of all detoxify the vegetables which you get from the market. Wash the vegetables properly and soak them in water for at least half an hour before cutting. By doing this all pesticides or any harmful bacteria is cleaned properly.

2.  When we eat lot of refined flour, cakes, pastries, tinned food or ear out or we consume junk food , our body can not digest it properly. We feel indigestion or bloated, our tongue remains coated, we have constipation or liver becomes sluggish. All these are symptoms of having mild toxins in the body. If we do not take them out they get collected in the body and start damaging our system and immunity. we should not let our liver be sluggish. We should include and eat lot of salads, fruits and leafy vegetables. Carrots and beetroot are rich in anti oxidants and carotene. They also have cleansing qualities. Seafood is rich in amino acids and taurine, which help liver to through toxins out of our body.

3.  We should have lot of fluids and water. Water keeps our kidneys clean. Consuming lukewarm water also helps in removing toxins from our system.

4.  We should keep fast once a week, so that our system is at rest. During fasting our body is restored. There are less fats in the blood and blood thins down, oxygen and nutrients are absorbed better and we feel rejuvenated. We can keep one day fast or three day fast, whatever suits the systems. If one can not

fast, then he/she should make changes in daily food habits.

5.  Include lot of fiber, leafy vegetables in your food. Drink lot of water. Avoid fats, fried stuff, cheese, ghee, red meat, pork, refined food, junk food etc.

6.  Exercise is another way of detoxifying. During exercise we sweat through our skin. Exercise should be done early morning or three hours after we have had our food (meals). Otherwise it will do us harm.

7.  Juices and herbal tea are also very good for detoxing. Herbal tea such as jasmine, tulasi, mint, ginger, rose and chamomile is very good. Coconut water, fruit juice, vegetables juices, lime water or luke warm water are boon for good heath and keep toxins away from body.

 CHAPTER 11
# Life style diseases

> "He who cures a disease may be the skillfullest, but he that prevents it is the safest physician."
>
> **— Thomas Fuller**

In this Chapter we will talk about foods and how they can prevent certain ailments. The most important thing is to keep acid and alkaline balance in our body. Also keep bowel movement proper. These two things will keep almost all ailments away from us. But the problem is that once the doctors say that there is no cure for certain ailment, people start believing and stop looking for other alternate treatments which may cure them.

1.  **Blood clotting:-** ' Everybody knows it is not cholesterol that kills you. It is the blood clot that forms on the top of the cholesterol-hardened plaque in the arteries that can be deadly.'

    **Dr David Kritchevsky, Wistar institute, Philadelphia.**

    Garlic, ginger, onions, black mushrooms (Chinese), clove, green tea, olive oil, fish and fish oil, grapes, red wine, red chillies and pepper. Garlic should not be cut, it should be crushed as crushing releases enzymes which are beneficial for us.

2. **Cold :-** Common cold taken 7 days to get cleared up. The reason for common cold is weak immune system. So best thing is to strengthen your immune system. Foods rich in chilly, pepper, spices, mustard, vinegar are good to unblock stuffy nose. Garlic and onion are also mucokinetic. Hot soups are also good. Vitamin C in any form such as amla should be given to cure cold and cough. Ginger tea, tulsi tea, elderberry are good for immune system. Inhalation of eucalyptus oil gives relief.

3. **Constipation:-** The most common cause of constipation is lack of water intake and fiber. Constipation if not treated at the right time, can lead to haemorrhoids and tiny anal tears. This happens due to lack of moisture in stool, that is why doctors suggest to have lot of water and fluids throughout the day. Foods that contain plenty of fiber are essential for fighting constipation, green leafy vegetables, whole wheat, lentils, salads, spinach, methi leaves, tomatoes should be made part of your diet. In fruits banana, papaya, figs, apricots, dates, bael fruit are very good to cure constipation. Avoid refined food. Do not ignore the urge to have bowel movement. Having boiled food only and no oil at all also leads to constipation in some cases.

4. **Eczema:-** Eczema is a form of skin disorder that affects the epidermis or outer layer of the skin. The skin becomes red with crusts, blisters, cracks and sometimes it starts. Heredity is one of the factors besides a sensitive immune system. often some foods worsen the condition. Milk, milk products such as cheese and curd, gluten in wheat, soya products, eggs can become causes of eczema. Deficiency

of omega 3 fatty acids in the diet can lower the immune system. We should have more of omega 3 fatty acids such as flax seeds, walnuts, grape seeds and sea foods. In fact we should have them daily. Vitamin A,C,E and selenium work wonder for eczema. Carrots, oranges, cherries, papaya, peaches are rich source of this vitamin. Tahe lot of greens and fruits. If you know that gluten in wheat causes eczema to you then switch on to rye, ragi, oats or jowar etc. along with all this, you must see a doctor for medicines.

> *Those who eat once a day are YOGIS, those who eat twice a day are BHOGI (lust) and those who eat thrice or more often are ROGI (sick).*

5. **Gout:-** when our body starts producing more amount of uric acid than it can handle or it is not able to eliminate uric acid, it starts accumulating it in our joints . in this condition our joints start swelling up and paining. Along with joints it also starts affecting our kidneys. Reason can be excessive alcohol, meat , oily and fries food .avoid all these foods to cure gout. Meat and alcohol are total no. Jowar and bajra are very useful because of their alkaline nature. Two fruits cherries and strawberries are very potent in the treatment of gout. Certain nutrients in these fruits prevent the uric acid from crystallizing and being deposited in joints. They also prevent inflammation. Walnut and almonds are rich in oils which reduce inflammation.

6. **Insomnia:-** There can be many reasons of sleeplessness, mental tension, overeating, not eating. Sometimes lack of calcium, B-complex vitamins, magnesium potassium and zinc also affects sleep

patterns. Avoid coffee, tea or any other such drink at night. Curd is very good for a nice sleep. Rice also induces sleep, so take diet consisting of rice and puses. Have hot milk at night before going to sleep. Milk contains tryptophan, an amino acid , which help increasing serotonin levels in the brain. Serotonin has calming effect on brain and induced sleep. make it a point not to sleep empty stomach if you are prone to sleep disorders.

7. **Psoriasis:-** The root cause of psoriasis is not known but, low immunity, liver dysfunction, low levels of hydrochloric acid in the body, faulty metabolism, improper digestion of the protein in the body can be a few causes of psoriasis. Even too much alcohol and meat consumption are also reasons which can really worsen the problem. Avoid acid forming foods such as tomato. Omega 3 fatty acids found in fish can help to some extent if the problem is not too bad. Fish oil flax seeds oil and evening primrose oil keeps the skin soft and avoids the formation of arachidonic acid, which makes psoriatic lesions turn red. One must have food rich in fiber. Include green in your diet as they are rich source of phytochemicals which repair the skin. Try to avoid stress as far as possible. In severe conditions must take medical help.

8. **Sinusitis:-** Light sinusitis stays for 10 to 15 days but in severe cases it can carry on for months and sometimes surgery is the only way out. Sinusitis can get triggered by any kind of allergy such as food allergy, dust allergy, food colours and pollen in plants. If you are affected by sinusitis let your nose be infection free. Do not let it block, let it free flowing. Lot of warm water with ginger, tulsi tea, hit soups are

good to treat sinusitis. Avoid mucus forming foods such as milk and milk products and wheat. Have juice of radish along with its leaves. This is age old remedy for sinus treatment. Spices, green chillies also help in this condition. Food rich in zinc, vitamin A and C should be taken. Try to make immune system strong by taking selenium and zinc.

9. **Varicose veins:-** Veins gets swollen up, red and enlarged due to too much pressure on them which may be because of pregnancy, obesity, standing for longer time, sedentary life style. They are removed surgically because it is difficult to treat them otherwise. Try not to get into this condition. But with proper food you can avoid the pain caused by them. Vitamin E rich food keeps the blood thin and improves circulation. Omega 3 rich food such as fish, it improves blood circulation, reduces inflammation and prevents blood clotting. All deep red coloured vegetables and fruits are good for varicose veins. Carrots, plums, beetroot are beneficial. Green tea, jamun and cherries contain anthocyanidins and proanthocyanidins which improve the tone of venous wall and prevents it from swelling and bleeding. Onion, garlic and ginger keep the veins soft by preventing clotting. Gingko biloba, zinc, and vitamin c enriched food is also helpful in this condition. Try not to gain weight at any cost.

"The food you eat can be either the safest and most powerful form of medicine or the slowest form of poison."

— *Ann Wigmore*

## Certain life style diseases

**Cholesterol / Heart diseases :-** The main cause of life style diseases is cholesterol. Cholesterol is essential for our body because with the help of cholesterol our body produces hormones, vitamin D and maintain the membranes of our cells. When it gets oxidized by free radicals it becomes harmful for us. There should be balance of two main types of cholesterol HDL and LDL which are High Density Lipoprotein( bad cholesterol) and Low Density Lipoprotein( good cholesterol). LDL is high in fatty acids and low in protein and more prone to oxidation. Food devoid of antioxidants such as vitamins A,C,E and selenium oxidizes LDL thus making it bad for the health. HDL is low in fatty acids and high in protein. It transports the extra cholesterol left by LDL back to liver and tissues. So balance in both type of cholesterol should be there.

It is not that vegetarians are not prone to cholesterol diseases such as heart problems, if they are having animal fat like milk, paneer, cheese, white flour they too can get affected by LDL. Meat, dairy products, oils, stress and many other things are responsible for LDL. Green vegetables and diet rich in fiber should be consumed to avoid LDL. Otherwise it will damage our arteries.

## What to eat:-

**Olive oil:-** The most potent oil for any type of cholesterol. It lowers LDH, raises HDL a liitle. It has been declared as best oil among others because they lower both LDL and HDL. Studies by university of California's D Daniel Steinberg find that olive oil is very potent in thwarting toxin oxidation of LDL cholesterol.

**Beans:-** Beans are very good to keep cholesterol under check. All types of beans kidney,soya, french, navy, black,pinto are good for us. 150 to 200gm of beans in one day are potent to keep LDL under check.

**Garlic:-** Garlic has been named as wonder herb. Whether raw , cooked or pickled it is good in any form. Consuming two small cloves ( not the big bulb) every day makes lot of difference. This is my own experience. It also thins the blood and does not let the blood form clots. L.T.M Medical college Mumbai, Bastyr college of Seattle has done some experiences with garlic and they also have found same results.

**Oats:-** Long back Dutch scientists revealed the power of oats 'a small bowl (55gm) of oats taken daily can keep the levels of cholesterol balanced. Oats contain beta glucans, a sort of soluble fiber which gels in intestines. This helps in removing extra cholesterol from bloodstream. Oats with its bran is much better than oats which are without bran.

**Onion:-** Onion especially raw is very potent in boosting levels of HDL cholesterol. It is age old folklore medicine just like garlic. Though cooked onion looses some of its properties but never the less that is also good. Onion can be consumed with lunch or dinner and to avoid its pungent smell have cardamom after eating onion. Onion also protect from sun stroke.

**Fish:-** Fish is very good as it contains omega 3 fatty acids which are helpful in uplifting HDL. Fish which are fat such as salmon, mackerel, herring, tuna are able to help boost levels of HDL effectively. Salmon also lowers triglycerides .

**Almonds and walnuts:-** Both are rich in monounsaturated fats which reduce cholesterol levels and LDL. Almonds are very good for brain development also. Walnuts generate heat so they should be consumed in moderation and not too much. Have 8 to 9 almonds and one or two walnuts daily.

**Flax seeds:-** Must take 2 to 4 tea spoons of flax seeds everyday to increase HDL.

**Carrots, grapefruits, strawberry, apples, all are very good for keeping cholesterol levels low.**

> *There are a few food items such as salt, sugar and fat which one should consume in moderation, infact lesser the better.*

**Diabetes:-** Food which we eat is turned into glucose and transformed into energy. Pancreas make insulin which help glucose enter the cells of our body. Glucose is the main fuel for the cells in our body. When our body is not able to produce insulin , glucose get accumulate in the body and its level goes up and a person becomes diabetic. So ineffectiveness of insulin is the real cause of diabetes. We should try to keep insulin under check.

There are certain foods that affect diabetes. One should avoid these food items . These foods contains certain elements which stimulate the potency of insulin. Sometimes they act directly to regulate blood sugar. Diabetes does happen over night. It takes long time to develop. If you have a family history of diabetes, you can always avoid the onset of this disease by avoiding food which can lead to diabetes. Obesity is a threat to diabetes. if you are normal weight and have insulinsensivity , be careful. Insulin resistence is generally inherited and on getting perfect environment such as food, it is triggered .

**Karela (bittergourd):-** Fresh karela juice which is very better is very effective in diabetes. it should be consumed early morning, empty stomach. It reduces the levels of blood sugar. It also purifies blood, treats piles and boils. Karela is good for immune system and carbohydrate metabolism.

**Jamun ( Jambool):-** Every part of jamun has medicinal value. Jamun as a fruit is eaten raw, its seed is used in powered form in the treatment of diabetes. jamun removes toxins from the body especially liver. It is good for liver and pancreas. It is ancient tradition medicine in India.

**Methi (Fenugreek):-** Methi is very effective in the treatment of diabetes. Soak a spoonful of methi seeds at night and early morning have that water along with seeds. Or boil them and consume only water. Green methi can also be taken as vegetable. Methi is effective in bringing down triglycerides. It is useful in aneamia. Methi should be cooked in mustard oil to get more benefits.

**Amla (Indian Gooseberry):-** It is one of the richest sources of vitamin C. known as an immunity booster, it is a laxative, good for skin ailments and potent in clearing skin. taken raw or as a murabba its qualities remain, but the moment you boil it , the benefits go down. It can be consumed in juice form.

**Fiber :-** One must make it a habit to have fiber rich diet since childhood so that many of the ailments can be kept at bay. Have lot of vegetables and fruits. Consume all the cereals such as wheat, jowar, bajra, soya, nacchi, ragi etc. Fiber removes toxins and waste product from the body. It also lowers cholesterol levels and controls our appetite. It is good for diabetic people because it controls blood sugar levels. It lowers cholesterol and reduces the risk of heart problems.

## Obesity:-

A person who weighs more than 10 kg above his/her normal weight falls in the category of obese persons. Once you put on weight and become obese it becomes very very difficult to shed it. There can be many reasons for the obesity. Foods which is not digested properly gets stored as fat in the body. Sometimes lack of exercise, wrong food habits, hormone imbalance, insulin utilization are also the reason for being obese. If thyroid is not functioning properly it affects body weight. If insulin level is high in body it helps in storage of fat in body. Any kind of hormonal imbalance also affects our body weight. Obesity can lead to diabetes. Develop good food habits.

Increase fiber intake. Have fresh green vegetables and antioxidant rich food. Have plenty of water. Avoid refined food and fried snacks. Switch over to buffalo milk. Do not take too much meat, pork and chicken, rather have fish. Must have 3-4 types of fruits in a day. Have more of soya in any form. Eat seeds and nuts in moderation. Do exercise regularly. Take the toxins out of your body with the help of herbs and diet. Give good nourishment to yourself and improve your metabolism. Develop good food habits. Do walking regularly. Obesity can lead to diabetes.

> *Any food item which has shelf life more than 24 hours, is not fresh food. There may be chemicals added to keep it for a longer period. The more longer shelf life , more chemical added food it becomes.*

## Some foods you say no to:-

### Sugar:-

When sugars bond with proteins they attract other proteins which form a sticky weblike substance. This weblike substance plays great role in blocking our arteries and stiffening our joints. It also webs our clear tissues such as lens of eye which leads to cataract. In diabetics it speads up. Sugar is poison for us its consumption should be restricted. We all know about it but we hardly follow this.

Sugar hinders the ability of adrenal glands to control stress hormones. So stop having more sugar.

### Refined Flour:-

Do not eat refined flour/maida. If you remember during our childhood we were taught how to make glue from maida and water. This maida gets stuck to the walls of our intestines. If we eat it regularly , it remains there and leads to constipation . Later on it start giving stomach related problems including colon cancer.

### Some points to remember:-

• Exercise regularly or go for regular walks.

• Eat lot of green vegetables and fruit.

- Eat complex carbohydrates and avoid refined carbs.

- Avoid meat and switch over to fish.

- Switch to mono-unsaturated oils such as olive oil, ground nut oil etc.

- Avoid stress.

- Alcohol should be avoided as it is harmful to adrenal glands.

- Caffeine can raise stress hormones in some people. It does not suit everybody